The Night of the Eternal Moon

Fairy tales, Folk tales, Legends & Mythology, Volume 12

Patrick William Lee

Published by B&H Publishing Group, 2024.

This is a work of fiction. Similarities to real people, places, or events are entirely coincidental.

THE NIGHT OF THE ETERNAL MOON

First edition. September 6, 2024.

ISBN: 979-8224464074

Written by Patrick William Lee.

Table of Contents

To those who walk between the shadows and the light,

May you always find the courage to face the unknown,

The strength to make impossible choices,

And the wisdom to see the beauty in the balance.

For the dreamers, the believers, and the quiet heroes—

This is your story too.

Chapter 1: The Prophecy of the Eternal Moon

The village of Elderglen lay nestled in a secluded valley, hidden from the rest of the world by dense forests and towering mountains. The people of Elderglen were simple folk, their lives marked by the rhythm of the seasons, the cycles of the moon, and the ancient traditions passed down through generations. For as long as anyone could remember, the village had lived in relative peace, untouched by the conflicts and turmoil that plagued the lands beyond the mountains. But beneath the surface of this tranquil existence, a forgotten prophecy lay dormant, waiting for the right moment to awaken.

Elara sat by the hearth in her family's modest cottage, staring into the crackling flames. The warm glow of the fire danced across her face, but her thoughts were far from the comforting warmth of her home. For days now, she had felt a strange unease, a restlessness that gnawed at the edges of her mind. It was as if the very air around her had changed, charged with an invisible energy that she couldn't quite name.

"Something is coming," she whispered to herself, her voice barely audible over the crackling fire.

Her mother, Karia, glanced up from her sewing, her sharp eyes narrowing at her daughter's words. "What did you say, Elara?"

Elara hesitated for a moment, unsure whether to speak her thoughts aloud. She had always been a dreamer, prone to flights of fancy that her mother often dismissed as the musings of a young girl with too much imagination. But this time, the feeling was different. It wasn't a dream or a passing fancy—it was something deeper, something ancient and powerful.

"I... I don't know," Elara replied, shaking her head. "It's just a feeling. Like there's something in the air. Like something is about to change."

Karia's expression softened, but there was a hint of concern in her eyes. "You've always been a sensitive one, Elara. But don't let your imagination run wild. The world is full of strange things, but that doesn't mean they're all coming for us. We have our lives here, our village. That's what matters."

Elara nodded, though the unease in her chest remained. She knew her mother was trying to comfort her, but there was something in the air, something undeniable. The moon had been hanging lower in the sky lately, its silvery glow casting long shadows over the village, even during the day. Animals had been acting strangely—wolves howling at odd hours, birds migrating out of season, and the forests seemed quieter than usual, as though the very trees were holding their breath.

She had asked the village elder, Darien, about it a few days ago, but he had merely shaken his head and muttered something about the whims of nature. Still, she couldn't shake the feeling that there was more to it than that. Something was coming—something old, something powerful.

Later that evening, after her mother had gone to bed, Elara slipped out of the cottage and into the cool night air. The village was quiet, the only sounds the distant rustling of leaves and the soft chirping of crickets. The sky above was clear, and the moon—larger and brighter than she had ever seen it—hung like a sentinel in the heavens, its pale light washing over the village.

She made her way to the edge of the village, where the trees of the forest loomed like silent guardians. There, at the foot of an ancient oak, sat the village's most sacred relic—a stone altar carved with runes so old that even the village elders could not decipher them. It was said that the altar had been there long before the village had been founded, a remnant of a time when gods and spirits walked the earth.

Elara knelt before the altar, her fingers tracing the worn carvings. As a child, she had often come here to play, imagining herself as a great adventurer or a wise priestess communing with the gods. But tonight, the altar felt different. The air around it seemed to hum with energy, and the runes glowed faintly in the moonlight, as though they were trying to speak.

"Elara..." A voice, soft and whispering, drifted through the air, barely audible over the wind.

Elara froze, her heart pounding in her chest. She looked around, but there was no one there. The village was far behind her, and the forest was still.

"Elara…"

The voice came again, this time clearer, more insistent. It was a woman's voice, familiar yet strange, as though it had been carried across the ages. Elara stood slowly, her eyes scanning the forest for the source of the voice.

"Who's there?" she called, her voice trembling slightly.

There was no response, only the soft rustling of the wind through the trees. But Elara could feel it now—something was watching her, something ancient and powerful. She took a step back from the altar, her pulse quickening.

"Elara… you must listen."

The voice came again, this time from within her own mind. Elara gasped, her hand flying to her chest. She had heard the stories—tales of the old gods, long forgotten by mortals, who could speak through dreams and visions. But those were just stories… weren't they?

"I don't understand," Elara whispered, her voice barely audible.

"The Eternal Moon approaches," the voice said, soft but firm. "It will bring with it great power—and great danger. You have been chosen, Elara. You must restore the balance."

Elara's mind raced, trying to make sense of the words. The Eternal Moon… she had heard that phrase before, in the old stories told around the hearth. It was said to be a celestial event, a night when the moon would remain in the sky for days, casting its light over the world and bringing with it magic and chaos. But it was just a myth—a story told to frighten children.

"Chosen for what?" Elara asked, her voice trembling. "I don't understand. What am I supposed to do?"

"The balance must be restored," the voice replied. "The old gods stir, and with them comes the end of the world as you know it. The Eternal Moon will bring the gods back to the mortal realm—but if the balance is not restored, they will bring ruin. You must find the Moonstone and return it to its rightful place. Only then can the balance be maintained."

Elara's heart pounded in her chest. The Moonstone… another relic from the old stories. It was said to be a powerful artifact, one that could control the very forces of the moon itself. But no one had seen it for centuries, and many believed it was nothing more than legend.

"I don't even know where to find the Moonstone," Elara said, her voice rising with desperation. "How can I stop something like this?"

"You will not be alone," the voice replied, softer now, almost soothing. "Others will come to your aid. But you must be strong, Elara. The fate of your world depends on it."

The wind picked up, rustling the leaves in the trees, and the glow of the runes on the altar faded. Elara stood frozen for a moment, her mind reeling from what she had just experienced. The voice was gone, but the weight of its words lingered.

The Eternal Moon. The old gods returning to the world. The Moonstone.

It couldn't be real... could it?

She turned and hurried back to the village, her heart racing. She needed to speak to Elder Darien. He had lived in the village for longer than anyone, and if anyone knew the truth about the old stories, it was him. If the Eternal Moon was coming—and if the prophecy was real—she needed answers.

ELDER DARIEN'S COTTAGE was small and unassuming, tucked away at the far edge of the village. Elara knocked on the door, her pulse still pounding in her ears. After a moment, the door creaked open, and the elder's weathered face appeared in the doorway.

"Elara?" he said, his voice rough with age. "What are you doing here at this hour? Is something wrong?"

"I need to talk to you," Elara said, her voice urgent. "It's about the Eternal Moon."

Darien's eyes widened slightly, but he said nothing. He stepped aside, gesturing for her to enter.

Elara stepped into the dimly lit cottage, her heart still racing. Darien motioned for her to sit by the hearth, where a small fire crackled softly. He lowered himself into the chair opposite her, his expression grave.

"The Eternal Moon..." he murmured, his voice low. "I haven't heard anyone speak of that in many years. It's an old story, one most have forgotten."

"I think it's real," Elara said, her voice barely above a whisper. "I... I heard a voice. It told me that the Eternal Moon is coming, and that the old gods are returning. It said I've been chosen to restore the balance."

Darien's brow furrowed, and he leaned forward, his eyes studying her intently. "A voice? Whose voice?"

"I don't know," Elara admitted. "It was a woman's voice, but it felt... ancient. Like it came from somewhere far away."

Darien was silent for a long moment, his gaze distant. Finally, he spoke. "The Eternal Moon is more than just a story, Elara. It is a prophecy—a warning left to us by the ancients. The moon will remain in the sky for three days and three nights, and during that time, the old gods will walk the earth once more. Their power will return, and with it, chaos."

Elara's heart sank. It was true, then. The prophecy was real.

"But why me?" she asked, her voice trembling. "Why have I been chosen?"

Darien sighed, leaning back in his chair. "I cannot say for certain, but there is an old belief that the Eternal Moon will only come when the world has lost its balance—when the connection between mortals and the divine has been severed. Perhaps you have been chosen because you possess something that can restore that balance."

"The Moonstone," Elara whispered.

Darien's eyes widened slightly, and he nodded. "Yes. The Moonstone is said to be the key to controlling the Eternal Moon's power. But it was lost long ago, hidden away in the mountains beyond the forest. Many have sought it, but none have returned."

Elara's mind raced. The mountains beyond the forest... it was a dangerous journey, one that few had ever attempted. But if the prophecy was real—if the Eternal Moon was coming—she had no choice.

"I have to find it," she said, her voice firm. "I have to stop the Eternal Moon before it brings ruin to the world."

Darien studied her for a long moment, his expression unreadable. Finally, he nodded. "If what you say is true, then you may be our only hope. But be warned, Elara—this journey will not be easy. The forces you will face are beyond anything you have ever known."

"I'm not afraid," Elara replied, though her heart trembled with fear. "I have to do this."

Darien nodded again, a flicker of respect in his eyes. "Then may the gods watch over you."

As Elara left Darien's cottage and stepped back into the cool night air, the weight of her decision settled heavily on her shoulders. The prophecy of the Eternal Moon was real, and she had been chosen to prevent it from bringing destruction to her world.

But the path ahead was uncertain, and she knew that the journey to find the Moonstone would be fraught with danger. Still, she couldn't turn back now. The fate of the world depended on her.

She glanced up at the sky, where the moon hung heavy and low, its light casting long shadows over the village. For a moment, she thought she saw something—a figure, tall and shadowy, standing at the edge of the forest, watching her.

She blinked, and the figure was gone.

Elara's heart raced, but she pushed the fear aside. She had a mission, and she couldn't afford to be afraid.

The Night of the Eternal Moon was coming.

And Elara would be ready.

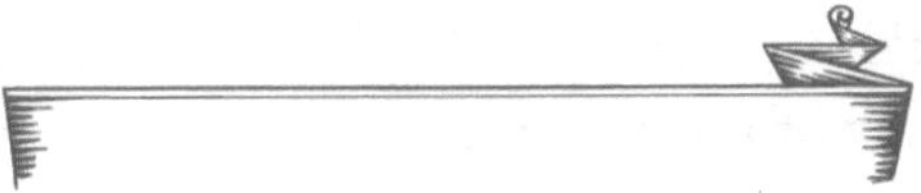

Chapter 1: The Prophecy of the Eternal Moon

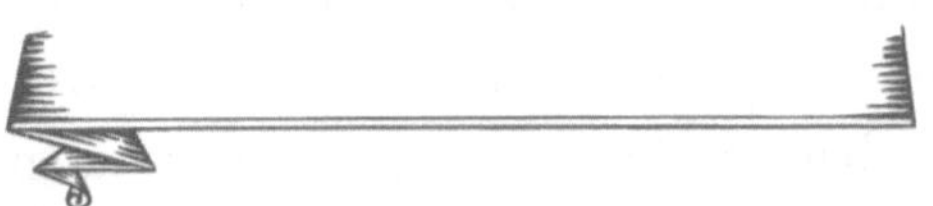

The sun dipped below the jagged mountains surrounding Elderglen, casting long shadows across the village and tinting the sky a dusky pink. Evening had come swiftly, but the air was thick with a strange tension that Elara could feel in her bones. The village, usually bustling with activity in the hours before dusk, was eerily quiet. Even the animals seemed unsettled—the goats that grazed on the hills shifted nervously, their ears twitching, and the birds that usually sang their evening songs were silent.

Elara sat on the stone steps of her family's small cottage, her hands resting on her knees as she gazed out at the darkening sky. She couldn't shake the feeling that something was wrong, something much larger than the usual worries of daily life. It had started a few weeks ago, with the animals behaving strangely—dogs barking at empty air, cats hissing at shadows, and birds flying in erratic patterns. The villagers had whispered among themselves, blaming the heat or the changing seasons, but Elara knew better.

There was something more to it—something ancient and foreboding.

Her mother had been dismissive when she'd mentioned it. Karia was practical, a woman of the earth who believed in what she could see and touch. Legends and prophecies, she had always said, were the stuff of stories, meant to entertain children and keep them from wandering too far into the woods. But Elara had always been drawn to those stories, fascinated by the idea that there were greater forces at play in the world than what could be explained by simple logic.

And now, the tales of the Eternal Moon were creeping back into the conversations of the villagers.

"Elara!" Her mother's voice called from inside the cottage, jolting her from her thoughts.

Elara stood quickly and brushed the dirt from her dress before stepping inside. The warm glow of the fire greeted her, and the familiar scent of stew wafted through the air. Karia was at the hearth, stirring a pot, her back to Elara.

"You'll catch a chill sitting out there at night," Karia said without turning around. "These autumn nights are colder than they seem."

Elara smiled faintly. Her mother had always been overprotective, ever since her father had died when she was a child. She had taken on the role of both parents, working tirelessly to provide for Elara and keep their small home in order.

"I was just thinking," Elara replied, moving to the table and sitting down.

"Thinking about what?" Karia asked, glancing over her shoulder with a raised eyebrow.

"The stories," Elara said softly. "About the Eternal Moon."

Karia sighed, turning back to the pot. "Not that again, Elara. You've been listening to too many of the old folks' tales."

"But what if they're true?" Elara pressed, leaning forward slightly. "What if the Eternal Moon is real, and it's coming? The animals have been acting strange, and the sky... it feels different."

Karia waved her hand dismissively. "The animals are always acting strange this time of year. They can sense the change in the weather. It's nothing more than that."

Elara bit her lip, her fingers nervously playing with the edge of her sleeve. She had always felt a connection to the old stories, but lately, they felt less like tales and more like warnings. The idea of the Eternal Moon—a night when the moon would remain in the sky for days, casting a magical glow over the world—had always fascinated her. According to the legends, it was during the Eternal Moon that the gods would walk among mortals once more, bringing with them great power, but also great danger.

"I know you don't believe in those stories," Elara said after a moment, "but what if there's some truth to them? What if the Eternal Moon is more than just a legend?"

Karia sighed again, this time more softly, and set the wooden spoon down. She turned to face Elara, her expression softening. "I'm not saying the stories don't hold some meaning. Every tale has a lesson. But the world we live in now...

it's not the same as the one from the stories. The gods haven't walked among mortals in a thousand years."

Elara nodded, though she wasn't convinced. The gods might not have walked among them in her lifetime, but that didn't mean they were gone.

"I just... I feel like something's coming," Elara said quietly, her gaze dropping to the table. "I can't explain it, but it's like the world is holding its breath."

Karia walked over and placed a hand on Elara's shoulder, her touch gentle but firm. "You've always had a vivid imagination. That's a gift. But don't let it make you fearful of things you can't control. Whatever's out there, we'll face it like we always have—together."

Elara smiled faintly and nodded. Her mother always knew how to bring her back to the present, to remind her that the world was full of uncertainties, but that they would always face them head-on.

Later that night, after the fire had burned low and the cottage was quiet, Elara lay in bed, staring up at the wooden beams of the ceiling. Sleep eluded her, her mind too busy with thoughts of the Eternal Moon and the strange happenings around the village. Finally, unable to lie still any longer, she slipped out of bed and tiptoed to the door.

The night air was crisp and cool, and Elara wrapped her shawl tightly around her shoulders as she stepped outside. The village was dark, save for a few faintly glowing lanterns hanging from doorways. The stars twinkled brightly above, but it was the moon that caught Elara's attention.

It hung low in the sky, larger than usual, its pale light casting long shadows across the ground. But there was something strange about it—something almost... unnatural. The light was too bright, too intense, and as Elara stared at it, she felt a chill run down her spine.

"Elara?" A voice called from the shadows, startling her.

Elara turned quickly to see Darien, the village elder, approaching from the path that led to the village's archives. He was an old man, with a long white beard and kind eyes that always seemed to hold a wealth of knowledge.

"What are you doing out here at this hour?" he asked, his voice gentle.

"I couldn't sleep," Elara admitted. "Something about the moon... it feels wrong."

Darien followed her gaze to the sky and nodded slowly. "You've always had a keen sense for these things."

Elara hesitated for a moment before speaking again. "I've been thinking about the stories. The ones about the Eternal Moon. Do you think it's possible that the prophecy could be real?"

Darien didn't respond immediately. Instead, he turned and began walking toward the village's small archive building, motioning for Elara to follow.

Inside, the archive was dimly lit by a single candle, casting flickering shadows on the rows of dusty old books and scrolls that lined the shelves. Darien led her to the far corner, where an old leather-bound book lay open on a wooden table.

"This is one of the oldest records we have," Darien said, his voice low. "It speaks of the Eternal Moon, and the prophecy that accompanies it."

Elara's heart skipped a beat as she approached the book, her eyes scanning the faded text. The pages were yellowed with age, and the writing was in an ancient script, but she could make out enough to understand its meaning.

"The Night of the Eternal Moon will come when the balance between the mortal and divine realms has been broken," Darien read aloud. "During this time, the moon will remain in the sky for three days and three nights, and the gods will return to the world of mortals. But with their return will come chaos, as the old powers seek to reclaim what was once theirs."

Elara felt a chill run down her spine as she listened. The words seemed to echo the feelings of unease that had been building inside her for weeks.

"Does anyone else know about this?" she asked, her voice barely above a whisper.

Darien shook his head. "Few people take these old prophecies seriously anymore. Most believe they're nothing more than stories, warnings from a time when the gods were more present in the world. But I've seen things—signs—that suggest the prophecy may be more than just a tale."

Elara's heart raced. "What kind of signs?"

"The animals," Darien replied, his brow furrowing. "The way they've been behaving—restless, agitated. It's as if they can sense something coming. And the sky... you've noticed it, haven't you? The moon has been brighter, larger, hanging lower in the sky."

Elara nodded, her mind racing. "I've felt it too. Like the world is... shifting."

Darien nodded slowly, his eyes thoughtful. "There are forces at play that we don't fully understand. The prophecy speaks of a chosen one—a mortal who will be called upon to restore the balance between the realms. If the Eternal Moon is coming, that person will have a great role to play."

Elara felt her breath catch in her throat. Could it be possible? Could she be that person?

"But how would I know?" she asked, her voice trembling. "How would I know if I've been chosen?"

Darien smiled faintly, his gaze softening. "The gods have a way of making themselves known, Elara. If you are meant to play a role in this, you will feel it. You've always had a connection to the old stories, a curiosity that others lack. Perhaps that's the first sign."

Elara swallowed hard, her mind whirling with possibilities. She had always felt drawn to the legends of the gods, always wondered what it would be like if they returned to the world. But now, the idea of being chosen to play a part in that return was overwhelming.

"What should I do?" she asked, her voice barely above a whisper.

Darien was silent for a long moment, his gaze distant. Finally, he spoke. "For now, watch and listen. The Eternal Moon hasn't risen yet, but when it does, you'll know. And when that time comes, you must be ready."

Elara nodded, though her heart pounded with fear and uncertainty. The weight of the prophecy, the possibility of being chosen, felt like a heavy burden on her shoulders.

As she left the archive and stepped back into the cool night air, the village was quiet, and the moon still hung low in the sky, casting its eerie glow over the land. Elara gazed up at it, her mind racing with the knowledge she had just gained.

The Night of the Eternal Moon was approaching.

And with it, her destiny.

Elara spent the next few days in a state of restless anticipation. The strange omens continued—birds flying in erratic patterns, animals behaving oddly, and the sky glowing faintly at night. The villagers whispered among themselves, but few seemed to take the signs seriously. To them, it was just another strange season, one that would pass like all the others.

But Elara knew better. The weight of the prophecy loomed over her like a storm cloud, and she couldn't shake the feeling that something monumental was about to happen. Each night, she found herself drawn to the altar at the edge of the village, where she would sit and stare at the moon, waiting for some sign, some clue as to what her role in all of this would be.

One evening, as she sat by the altar, the wind picked up, rustling the leaves in the trees. The moon hung low in the sky, its pale light casting long shadows across the ground. Elara shivered, though the air was not particularly cold.

And then, she heard it again.

"Elara..."

The voice was soft, barely a whisper, but it sent a jolt of recognition through her. She stood quickly, her heart pounding in her chest, and scanned the forest around her.

"Elara... you must listen."

The voice came again, this time clearer, more insistent. It was the same voice she had heard before—the voice that had spoken to her at the altar.

"What do you want from me?" Elara called, her voice trembling. "What am I supposed to do?"

"The Eternal Moon is coming," the voice replied, soft but firm. "You must be ready."

Elara swallowed hard, her heart racing. "How? How do I prepare for something like this?"

"You will find the answers," the voice whispered. "The path is before you."

And then, just as quickly as it had come, the voice was gone, leaving Elara standing alone in the darkness, the moon's pale light washing over her.

The Eternal Moon was coming. The prophecy was real.

And Elara's journey was about to begin.

Chapter 2: The First Sign

The days following Elara's encounter with the strange voice were filled with an anxious stillness, a tension that gripped the village of Elderglen. As though the very air had thickened, it became harder to breathe, harder to think. Everything felt off balance. Even the sun, as it hung in the sky, seemed dimmer, its rays unable to dispel the lingering dread that settled over the land. The villagers whispered among themselves, their eyes darting nervously toward the forest as though expecting something to emerge from the shadows at any moment.

Elara, too, felt the change. Though she went about her daily chores as usual—gathering firewood, tending the garden, and helping her mother—her mind was constantly on edge, watching for the first sign of the prophecy she knew was coming. The voice had told her to be ready, but she still had no idea what that meant. How could she be ready for something she couldn't even begin to understand?

The first sign, when it finally came, was unexpected.

It began like any other day. Elara rose early to collect herbs from the edge of the forest. The forest had always been a place of peace for her, a sanctuary where she could lose herself in the quiet rustling of the leaves and the songs of the birds. But now, the forest seemed different. The trees, usually full of life, stood still and silent, their branches swaying only faintly in the breeze. Even the birds seemed quieter, their songs muffled and distant.

As she made her way through the underbrush, Elara felt a strange chill run down her spine. She paused, listening. There was something in the air, something that made the hair on the back of her neck stand on end.

And then she saw it.

High above the treetops, the sun, usually blazing brightly in the morning sky, was dimming. The light around her began to fade, as though a great shadow was slowly creeping across the heavens. Elara's heart quickened as she looked up, watching in awe as the sun began to disappear, swallowed by the dark shadow of the moon.

An eclipse.

But this was no ordinary eclipse. The sky darkened far more rapidly than it should have, the light vanishing so swiftly that within minutes, the day had turned to night. The once-clear sky was now pitch black, the sun completely obscured, leaving the land bathed in an eerie twilight. Elara's breath caught in her throat.

This was it—the first sign.

She dropped the basket of herbs she had been carrying and ran toward the village, her heart pounding in her chest. Her feet stumbled over rocks and roots as she sprinted through the forest, her mind racing with panic. She had to find Elder Darien—he would know what to do, what this meant. She had to tell him that the prophecy was starting, that the Eternal Moon was coming.

By the time she reached the village, the eclipse had deepened. The entire village was bathed in a strange, dusky glow, the light around them dull and unnatural. People were standing in the streets, staring up at the sky with wide, fearful eyes. The children clung to their mothers, and the elders whispered to each other, their faces pale with fear.

"Elara!" her mother's voice called from behind her.

Elara turned to see Karia running toward her, her expression frantic. "What's happening?" Karia asked, grabbing her daughter's arm. "Why has the sky gone dark?"

Elara swallowed hard, her mind spinning. She didn't know how to explain it. How could she tell her mother that the stories she had always dismissed as myths were coming true before their very eyes?

"I don't know," Elara lied, shaking her head. "But I think this is just the beginning."

Karia's grip on her arm tightened. "What do you mean?"

Before Elara could respond, a voice rang out from the center of the village. "Everyone! Gather in the square!"

It was Elder Darien. He stood near the well, his arms raised, calling for the villagers to come closer. The people of Elderglen hurried to obey, their faces full of fear and confusion. Elara and her mother joined the crowd, standing at the edge as Darien began to speak.

"We are witnessing a rare and powerful event," Darien said, his voice loud and clear. "This eclipse—though frightening—may be a natural occurrence. But there is no need for panic. We will wait it out together."

"But why is it lasting so long?" a voice called from the crowd. "It's been dark for over an hour!"

"An eclipse shouldn't last this long!" someone else shouted.

Darien held up his hands, trying to calm the crowd. "I understand your fear, but we must remain calm. We will—"

His words were cut off as a loud howl echoed through the village, reverberating off the stone walls of the cottages. Elara's heart leaped into her throat as she turned toward the sound. It was unlike anything she had ever heard—a deep, guttural howl, like that of a wolf, but much more sinister. The sound seemed to chill the air, and the villagers fell silent, their eyes wide with fear.

Another howl followed, then another, until the air was filled with the sound of howling creatures, coming from the direction of the forest.

"They're coming from the woods!" someone shouted.

Panic rippled through the crowd as people began to scramble toward their homes, grabbing their children and fleeing inside. Elara's mother grabbed her hand and pulled her toward their cottage, but Elara resisted, her eyes fixed on the edge of the forest.

"Elara, come!" Karia pleaded, her voice trembling. "We need to get inside!"

Elara nodded, but her feet remained rooted to the ground. Something was drawing her toward the forest, a pull that she couldn't explain. The howling had grown louder, closer, and though every instinct told her to run, she found herself taking a step toward the trees.

"Elara!" her mother called again, but her voice seemed distant, muffled by the strange sensation that was overtaking Elara.

And then she saw it.

Figures—shadowy and indistinct—moving between the trees at the edge of the village. At first, they were barely visible, like wraiths gliding through the fog. But as they drew closer, their forms became clearer. Tall, thin figures with glowing eyes that gleamed in the dim light of the eclipse. Their movements were slow, almost graceful, as they slipped between the trees, their eyes fixed on the village.

Elara's heart raced. These weren't animals. They weren't wolves or any other creatures of the forest.

These were something else.

"Elara!" Karia's voice finally broke through, and Elara felt herself pulled back to reality. She turned and ran after her mother, her heart pounding in her chest as they hurried into the cottage and slammed the door behind them.

Inside, the cottage felt suffocating. The small windows offered little light, and the air was thick with fear. Karia bolted the door, her face pale as she turned to her daughter.

"What were those things?" Karia whispered, her voice shaking. "What did you see?"

Elara's mind raced, but she couldn't find the words to explain what she had seen. The figures in the woods, the howling, the strange eclipse—it was all connected to the prophecy. She knew that now.

"It's starting," Elara whispered, more to herself than to her mother. "The prophecy... it's real."

Karia stared at her, her eyes wide with disbelief. "What are you talking about? What prophecy?"

Before Elara could respond, a loud crash came from the roof of the cottage, followed by the sound of something heavy landing outside. Karia gasped, her hand flying to her mouth.

"Elara, stay here," Karia whispered, grabbing a knife from the table. "I'll check the back."

"No!" Elara said quickly, grabbing her mother's arm. "We need to stay together. Whatever's out there—"

The crash came again, this time louder, and then a sound—a low, guttural growl—echoed through the walls of the cottage.

Elara's heart raced as she and her mother pressed themselves against the wall, their breath coming in shallow gasps. The growling grew louder, and then there was silence. For a moment, all they could hear was the sound of their own breathing, the stillness of the village outside.

And then, the door creaked open.

A figure stumbled inside, its shadow stretching across the floor in the dim light of the eclipse. Elara's breath caught in her throat as she saw it—a man, or what had once been a man, but now twisted and deformed. His skin was covered in fur, his face elongated like that of a wolf, and his eyes gleamed with a strange, wild light.

He collapsed onto the floor, panting heavily, blood dripping from a deep wound in his side.

"Elara, get back!" Karia hissed, raising the knife.

But the creature didn't move to attack. Instead, it lifted its head, its eyes locking onto Elara's with an intensity that sent a shiver down her spine.

"The gods..." the creature rasped, its voice barely audible through its labored breathing. "They are returning..."

Elara's heart pounded in her chest. She stepped forward, her fear momentarily forgotten as she knelt beside the wounded creature.

"What do you mean?" she asked, her voice trembling. "What are you talking about?"

The creature's eyes flickered, and it let out a low, pained growl. "The gods... they are coming back... to reclaim what is theirs. The prophecy... the Eternal Moon... it has begun."

Elara's breath caught in her throat. The creature was speaking of the prophecy—the same prophecy she had read about in the village archives, the same prophecy that had haunted her dreams. The eclipse, the strange figures in the forest—it was all part of the prophecy.

"You have been chosen," the creature rasped, its voice growing weaker. "You must stop them... before it's too late..."

Elara's mind raced, her heart pounding in her chest. Chosen? How could she be chosen for something like this? She was just a girl, living in a small village, far from the great cities and kingdoms of the world. How could she possibly stop the return of the gods?

Before she could ask any more questions, the creature's body shuddered, and with a final, pained breath, it went still. Elara stared down at the lifeless form, her mind spinning with fear and confusion.

"Elara..." Karia whispered, her voice trembling. "What is happening?"

Elara stood slowly, her legs shaking beneath her. "I don't know," she admitted, her voice barely above a whisper. "But I think we're about to find out."

That night, Elara couldn't sleep. The creature's final words echoed in her mind, haunting her. **You have been chosen.** But chosen for what? How could she possibly stop the return of the gods? The idea seemed impossible, overwhelming.

But deep down, Elara knew that the prophecy was real. The signs were all around her—the eclipse, the strange creatures in the forest, the howling that still echoed in her ears. And now, the first of the old gods was stirring, preparing to return to the world of mortals.

As she lay in bed, staring up at the ceiling, Elara felt a strange calm settle over her. She didn't know what the future held, but she knew one thing for certain: the Eternal Moon was coming, and the world would never be the same.

She had been chosen.

And her journey was only just beginning.

Chapter 3: The Guardians of the Moon

The village of Elderglen had returned to a tense semblance of normality after the night of the eclipse. Yet, the stillness in the air felt forced, a fragile calm hovering over the people as if they were all collectively holding their breath. Elara, however, couldn't shake the weight of the wounded creature's final words from her mind. The village may have resumed its routines, but she could see the unease in the eyes of the people, the way they glanced toward the forest with suspicion and dread.

The village elders, the supposed keepers of wisdom and tradition, had met earlier that morning to discuss the recent events. Elara had waited patiently, her heart heavy with expectation, hoping that they would take the omens seriously, that they would offer guidance about the prophecy she knew was unraveling around them. She had even thought that perhaps Elder Darien, who had seemed so understanding before, would advocate for her concerns.

But when she was summoned to the meeting, the elders had offered nothing but dismissive words.

Elder Maris, the most senior among them, shook his head wearily as she stood before the council in the village hall. His gray eyes, once sharp and full of wisdom, now seemed clouded with cynicism. "Elara, these are strange times, yes, but every unusual event doesn't point to the fulfillment of some ancient prophecy. We have lived through strange eclipses before, through seasons of drought and flood. This is no different."

"But the signs are there!" Elara insisted, her voice trembling with frustration. "The eclipse lasted far longer than it should have, and the howling in the forest—it wasn't natural. And the creature... it spoke of the old gods returning. We can't just ignore this!"

Elder Maris exchanged a glance with Darien, who sat silently to his left. Darien looked away, his expression unreadable.

"Elara," Maris said gently, as if speaking to a child. "The stories of the Eternal Moon are just that—stories. Tales from a time when the world was more superstitious, when people explained the unexplainable through myth and legend. You're a bright young woman, but you're letting your imagination run wild."

Elara clenched her fists at her sides, struggling to keep her voice steady. "This isn't my imagination. You all felt the shift in the air, the way the village has changed. You've seen the fear in the people's eyes. You can't tell me this is normal."

Elder Voss, the youngest of the council, frowned, his dark eyebrows drawing together. "We're not denying that strange things have been happening, but you must understand that we have to maintain order. If we indulge every fear and superstition, it will only create chaos. The village needs stability, not panic."

"And what if the prophecy is real?" Elara shot back, her voice rising with desperation. "What if the Eternal Moon is coming, and the old gods are returning to claim the world? If we do nothing, we could be walking into disaster."

Elder Maris sighed and leaned back in his chair. "There are no Guardians of the Moon, Elara. That's just a fairy tale. There is no secret group of protectors watching over the celestial order, waiting to stop the moon from destroying us. We must focus on practical matters—keeping the village safe, maintaining our crops, and preparing for the coming winter."

Elara's heart sank as she looked around the table at the elders, their faces resolute in their decision to dismiss her concerns. Even Darien, who had once seemed willing to listen to her, remained silent. He kept his gaze on the floor, avoiding her eyes.

"I see," Elara whispered, her voice tight with emotion. "You've already made up your minds."

Elder Maris gave her a sympathetic smile. "We have. Now, go home, Elara. There's no need to worry yourself over things that don't concern you."

Elara swallowed the bitter retort that rose in her throat and nodded stiffly. Without another word, she turned on her heel and left the hall, her footsteps echoing in the empty space behind her.

As Elara walked through the village square, her heart felt heavy with frustration and anger. How could they not see what was happening? How could they be so blind to the danger? She had always respected the village elders, trusted their wisdom, but now, it seemed they were more interested in maintaining the status quo than in facing the truth.

She reached the edge of the village, where the forest loomed like a dark wall of secrets. The trees seemed taller today, their shadows stretching farther, as if they were watching her. Elara stopped for a moment, staring into the depths of the forest, her mind racing.

The elders weren't going to help her. If she wanted answers, she would have to find them herself.

The Guardians of the Moon. The stories had always fascinated her as a child—mysterious protectors who were said to guard the balance between the mortal and divine realms. They were rumored to live in hidden sanctuaries, far from the eyes of men, watching over the celestial order and preventing the old gods from returning to wreak havoc on the world. But no one knew if they were real, or if they were just another part of the village's lore.

Elara had always believed there was truth in the stories, and now, she was certain of it. If the prophecy of the Eternal Moon was coming to pass, then the Guardians would know what to do. They had to.

Taking a deep breath, she tightened her cloak around her shoulders and stepped into the forest. The trees closed in around her, the air growing cooler as she made her way through the underbrush. The path she had traveled so many times before now seemed unfamiliar, the landscape shifting in the dim light filtering through the canopy. But Elara didn't falter. Her determination fueled her steps, pushing her forward despite the uncertainty that gnawed at her.

She didn't know where to find the Guardians, but she knew she had to try. The village may have dismissed the prophecy as superstition, but Elara couldn't shake the feeling that something terrible was coming. She had seen the first sign—the eclipse that lasted far longer than any in living memory. And the creature she had encountered, the one that had spoken of the gods returning... it had been real. She had felt its pain, its desperation.

The prophecy was real.

Hours passed as Elara ventured deeper into the forest, her feet carrying her along narrow, winding paths that twisted and turned through the dense trees. The sun had long since disappeared behind the clouds, leaving the forest bathed in a gray, muted light. She had no idea where she was going, but she trusted her instincts, following the subtle pull in her chest that guided her forward.

She had to find the Guardians.

As the sun began to sink below the horizon, casting long shadows across the forest floor, Elara found herself standing at the edge of a wide clearing. The trees parted here, revealing a stretch of land that seemed untouched by time. In the center of the clearing stood a tall, crumbling stone structure, half-hidden by vines and moss. It looked ancient, as if it had been standing for centuries, forgotten by the world around it.

Elara's heart quickened. This had to be it.

She approached the structure cautiously, her eyes scanning the surroundings for any sign of life. The air was still, the forest quiet, save for the occasional rustle of leaves in the breeze. As she drew closer, she saw that the structure was a shrine of some kind, its walls adorned with faded carvings and symbols that she didn't recognize. The entrance was partially collapsed, the stone worn smooth by years of exposure to the elements.

Taking a deep breath, Elara stepped inside.

The interior of the shrine was dim, the only light coming from the slivers of sunlight that filtered through the cracks in the ceiling. The air was cool and damp, and the smell of earth and moss filled her nose. The walls were covered in intricate carvings, depicting scenes of the moon and stars, of figures standing beneath the night sky with their arms raised in reverence. In the center of the room stood a stone pedestal, its surface smooth and polished, as if it had been recently tended to.

Elara approached the pedestal slowly, her heart pounding in her chest. There was something sacred about this place, something ancient and powerful. She could feel it in the air, in the very stone beneath her feet.

But as she reached out to touch the pedestal, a voice rang out from the shadows.

"I wouldn't do that if I were you."

Elara froze, her hand hovering just above the stone. She spun around, her eyes searching the dim light for the source of the voice.

A figure emerged from the darkness, stepping into the faint light that filtered through the cracks in the ceiling. It was a man, tall and broad-shouldered, with dark hair that fell in loose waves around his face. He wore a leather tunic and a cloak that was torn and frayed at the edges, and a sword hung at his side. His eyes, dark and sharp, were fixed on her with an intensity that made her heart skip a beat.

"Who are you?" Elara demanded, her voice steady despite the fear that churned in her stomach.

The man crossed his arms over his chest, his expression unreadable. "I could ask you the same thing."

"I'm looking for the Guardians of the Moon," Elara said, lifting her chin defiantly. "Do you know where I can find them?"

The man raised an eyebrow, a faint smirk tugging at the corner of his lips. "You think the Guardians are real?"

Elara's jaw tightened.

"I know they are."

The man studied her for a moment, his eyes narrowing as if he were trying to see into her soul. Then, with a sigh, he shook his head. "You're either very brave, or very foolish."

"Who are you?" Elara asked again, taking a step toward him. "Are you one of the Guardians?"

The man let out a low chuckle. "I'm no Guardian, but I've been looking for them too." He paused, his gaze flickering to the pedestal behind her. "And I think we're both closer than we realize."

Elara frowned, her eyes narrowing in suspicion. "Why are you looking for them?"

The man's smirk faded, replaced by a grim expression. "Because if we don't find them soon, the world as we know it will be torn apart."

Elara's heart skipped a beat. "You believe in the prophecy too?"

The man nodded, his expression serious. "I've seen the signs. The eclipse, the creatures stirring in the shadows... it's all happening, just as the old texts said it would." He glanced at her, his eyes sharp and calculating. "But if you're here looking for the Guardians, then you must already know that."

Elara hesitated, then nodded. "I've seen the signs too. And I know that the Eternal Moon is coming."

The man's gaze softened slightly, and he extended a hand toward her. "I'm Dorian," he said. "And it looks like we're in this together."

Elara stared at his hand for a moment, then slowly reached out and shook it. His grip was firm, his hand calloused from years of wielding a sword. There was something reassuring about his presence, a confidence that made her feel less alone in the overwhelming task that lay ahead.

"We need to find the Guardians," Elara said, releasing his hand. "They're the only ones who can stop this."

Dorian nodded. "Agreed. But first, we need to figure out where they've gone. If the stories are true, the Guardians have been in hiding for centuries."

Elara glanced around the shrine, her eyes lingering on the faded carvings on the walls. "There must be something here that can point us in the right direction."

Together, they began searching the shrine, their eyes scanning the walls for any clue, any sign that could lead them to the Guardians. The carvings were ancient, worn with time, but Elara could make out faint symbols—depictions of the moon, the stars, and figures standing beneath the night sky. One of the carvings caught her eye—an image of a woman holding a crescent moon in her hands, her face turned toward the heavens.

"This one," Elara murmured, her fingers tracing the outline of the carving. "I think this is it."

Dorian stepped beside her, his eyes narrowing as he studied the carving. "The Moon Mother," he said quietly. "One of the old gods. She was said to be the guardian of the night, the one who protected the balance between the realms."

Elara's heart raced. "Do you think she's connected to the Guardians?"

Dorian nodded slowly. "It's possible. The Moon Mother was always associated with the celestial order. If the Guardians were her followers, they would have left signs like this."

Elara stared at the carving, her mind racing. The Moon Mother. The Guardians. It was all connected.

"We need to find out more," Elara said, turning to face Dorian. "We need to find someone who knows the old ways, who can help us decipher the meaning behind this."

Dorian's expression darkened. "There's only one person who might know that much. But she's not easy to find."

"Who?" Elara asked.

"Ilyana," Dorian replied. "A healer, and one of the last people who still practices the old ways. She knows more about the old gods and the Guardians than anyone else. If anyone can help us, it's her."

"Where is she?" Elara asked, her heart quickening.

Dorian hesitated, his eyes flickering with uncertainty. "She's... well, she's not exactly fond of visitors. But I know where to find her."

Elara nodded. "Then we need to go to her. If the prophecy is real, we don't have much time."

Dorian gave her a grim smile. "Then let's not waste any more of it."

The journey to find Ilyana took them deep into the heart of the forest, where the trees grew so close together that the sunlight barely penetrated the canopy. The path was narrow and overgrown, the air thick with the scent of pine and damp earth. As they walked, Elara couldn't shake the feeling that they were being watched, that something—or someone—was following them.

"Are you sure she's out here?" Elara asked, glancing nervously at the dense underbrush.

Dorian nodded. "Ilyana doesn't trust many people, so she stays far from the villages. But she's out here. We're close."

After what felt like hours of walking, they finally reached a small clearing. In the center stood a simple wooden hut, its walls covered in ivy and moss. Smoke curled from the chimney, and the faint scent of herbs and burning wood filled the air.

"This is it," Dorian said, nodding toward the hut.

Elara's heart raced as they approached the door. She wasn't sure what to expect—what kind of person Ilyana would be, or how she would react to their request. But they had no choice. If they were going to stop the Eternal Moon, they needed her help.

Dorian knocked on the door, the sound echoing in the quiet clearing. For a moment, there was only silence. Then, slowly, the door creaked open.

A woman stood in the doorway, her silver hair cascading down her back like a waterfall of moonlight. Her eyes, pale and piercing, seemed to see straight through them. She was older than Elara had expected, but there was a strength in her presence that was undeniable.

"I know why you've come," Ilyana said, her voice soft but firm. "And I know what you seek."

Elara swallowed hard. "Can you help us?"

Ilyana's eyes flickered with a mixture of sadness and resolve. "I can help you," she said quietly. "But the path ahead will not be easy. The prophecy is already in motion, and the Guardians... they are not what they once were."

Elara's heart sank. "What do you mean?"

Ilyana stepped aside, motioning for them to enter the hut. "Come inside," she said. "There is much you need to know."

As Elara and Dorian stepped into the dimly lit hut, Elara couldn't shake the feeling that they were about to learn something that would change everything.

The Guardians of the Moon were real.

But what Ilyana was about to reveal would be far more than Elara had ever imagined.

Chapter 4: The Moonstone Cavern

The journey into the mountains was longer and far more perilous than Elara had anticipated. The air grew thinner as they ascended, biting cold winds tearing at their cloaks, and the jagged peaks loomed above them like the spires of a fortress built by forgotten gods. Every step felt heavier, the path narrower and more treacherous as the trio moved deeper into the wilderness, following the rough markings on the ancient map they had uncovered in Ilyana's hut.

Ilyana, the wise healer who had joined them on their quest, led the way, her eyes narrowed with determination as she scanned the uneven trail. Her silver hair, flowing like moonlight in the wind, was the only part of her that seemed untouched by the weight of their journey. Dorian, the skilled warrior Elara had met at the shrine, brought up the rear, his hand always resting on the hilt of his sword, ever watchful for threats.

Elara herself felt a mixture of trepidation and excitement. They were getting closer to the Moonstone, the artifact that could control or unleash the power of the Eternal Moon. It was said to have been hidden deep within the Moonstone Cavern, a place few had ever seen and even fewer had returned from. According to Ilyana, the Guardians of the Moon had once protected it, but now the cavern lay abandoned, its traps and illusions left in place to keep intruders out.

As they climbed higher, the landscape became more barren, the trees thinning until only patches of scrub and scattered boulders remained. The wind howled through the mountain passes, a constant reminder of the unforgiving terrain they had chosen to traverse.

Elara pulled her cloak tighter around her shoulders and glanced at Ilyana, who was studying the map as they reached a narrow ridge. "How much farther do you think it is?"

Ilyana folded the map and tucked it into her satchel. "Not far now. We should reach the entrance to the cavern before nightfall, assuming there are no more... surprises."

Dorian, ever the skeptic, let out a low grunt. "I don't like surprises."

"None of us do," Ilyana replied, giving him a pointed look. "But if we're to retrieve the Moonstone, we have no choice but to face whatever lies ahead."

Elara felt a shiver run down her spine at Ilyana's words. The Moonstone Cavern was not just a physical challenge. According to the legends, it was a place where the mind and heart were tested, where illusions could bend reality, and where only those with pure intentions could hope to survive. It was no wonder that few who entered ever returned.

As the sun began to dip below the horizon, casting a reddish glow over the mountains, they finally reached the entrance to the cavern. It was a narrow, jagged opening in the rock, barely visible beneath the shadow of a large overhanging cliff. The entrance was framed by ancient carvings, worn down by centuries of wind and weather, but still recognizable as symbols of the moon and stars.

"This is it," Ilyana said, her voice barely audible over the wind. "The Moonstone Cavern."

Elara stared at the dark entrance, her heart pounding in her chest. This was the moment they had been preparing for—the moment where their journey truly began.

"Are we ready for this?" Elara asked, her voice trembling slightly.

Dorian stepped forward, his expression grim. "We don't have a choice, do we? If the prophecy is coming to pass, we need that Moonstone."

Ilyana nodded, but her eyes were distant, as if she were already bracing herself for what was to come. "Be prepared for anything," she said quietly. "The Guardians were not merciful when they set the traps in this place. They wanted to ensure that only the worthy could reach the Moonstone."

With a deep breath, Elara followed Ilyana and Dorian into the cavern.

The air inside the Moonstone Cavern was thick and damp, the walls slick with moisture and covered in lichen that glowed faintly in the dim light. The narrow passageway they entered widened as they moved deeper, revealing a labyrinth of tunnels that twisted and turned in every direction. The sound of dripping water echoed through the cavern, creating an eerie, rhythmic melody that seemed to grow louder with each step they took.

Elara held a torch in one hand, its flickering light casting long, shifting shadows on the walls. She couldn't shake the feeling that they were being watched, though by what, she couldn't say. The cavern had a presence of its own, a kind of ancient awareness that made her skin crawl.

"This place feels... wrong," Dorian muttered, his voice low.

"It's the magic of the Guardians," Ilyana replied. "The Moonstone isn't just hidden—it's protected. The deeper we go, the stronger the illusions will become. Keep your wits about you."

Elara nodded, though her heart raced. She had heard stories of the cavern's illusions—how they could warp reality, tricking even the sharpest minds into losing their way. She tightened her grip on the torch, determined to stay focused.

They continued deeper, navigating the twisting tunnels with caution. The path was treacherous, the ground uneven and strewn with loose rocks that threatened to send them tumbling at any moment. As they descended further into the mountain, the air grew colder, and the walls of the cavern seemed to close in around them.

It wasn't long before they encountered the first of the traps.

They had reached a wide chamber, the walls lined with ancient carvings that depicted scenes of battle between the old gods and mortals. In the center of the room stood a raised platform, and on that platform rested a large, ornate chest.

Elara's heart skipped a beat. Could the Moonstone be inside?

Dorian stepped forward, his eyes narrowing as he studied the platform. "It seems too easy," he muttered.

"That's because it is," Ilyana said, her voice tense. "Look at the floor."

Elara followed her gaze and saw that the floor around the platform was covered in intricate patterns, carved into the stone. At first, she didn't recognize their significance, but then she realized—they were pressure plates. Step on the wrong one, and the trap would be triggered.

"It's a test," Ilyana continued. "We have to cross the floor without triggering the trap."

"Great," Dorian muttered, his hand resting on the hilt of his sword. "Any idea how we're supposed to do that?"

Elara stared at the patterns on the floor, her mind racing. "The carvings on the walls... they're scenes from the legends. Battles between mortals and the old gods." She moved closer to one of the walls, studying the images. "The Guardians must have left clues here. If we can figure out the sequence, we can find the safe path."

Ilyana nodded, her eyes scanning the carvings. "Look for anything that stands out. Symbols, markings—anything that seems connected to the Moonstone."

For what felt like an eternity, they studied the carvings in silence, searching for the key to unlocking the path. Elara's eyes darted from one image to the next, her mind working to piece together the puzzle.

Finally, she saw it—a symbol carved into the armor of one of the figures in the battle scene. It was a crescent moon, the same symbol that had been etched into the shrine they had found in the forest.

"There," Elara said, pointing to the symbol. "That's the key. The Moon Mother. She was the guardian of the celestial order."

Ilyana followed her gaze, her eyes narrowing. "You're right. The Moon Mother was always associated with protection and guidance. Her symbol must be the safe path."

Dorian nodded. "Then we follow the crescent moons."

Taking a deep breath, Elara stepped onto the first tile, the one marked with the crescent moon. The ground beneath her didn't shift, no trap was triggered. She exhaled in relief and motioned for the others to follow.

One by one, they moved across the floor, stepping only on the tiles marked with the crescent moon. Each step was a test of their resolve, their hearts pounding with the knowledge that one wrong move could spell disaster.

When they finally reached the platform, Elara let out a breath she hadn't realized she'd been holding.

They had made it.

Dorian approached the chest, his hand resting on the lid. "This better be it," he muttered, before lifting the lid.

Inside the chest, nestled on a bed of black velvet, lay the Moonstone.

It was unlike anything Elara had ever seen. The stone was a deep, iridescent blue, swirling with streaks of silver that seemed to glow from within. It pulsed with a faint light, as if alive with its own energy.

But there was something wrong.

As Elara moved closer, she saw it—the stone was cracked.

A thin, jagged line ran down the center of the Moonstone, splitting it in two. The glow that emanated from the stone flickered, unstable, as if the very power it held was beginning to unravel.

"This isn't right," Ilyana whispered, her eyes wide with fear. "The Moonstone... it's broken."

Elara's heart sank. "What does that mean?"

"It means the balance has already begun to shift," Ilyana replied, her voice shaking. "The Eternal Moon's power is growing. If the Moonstone is damaged, we may not be able to control it."

Dorian cursed under his breath, his hands clenched into fists. "So what do we do now?"

"We need to repair it," Ilyana said, her voice steady despite the fear in her eyes. "There's still time, but we have to move quickly. If we don't restore the Moonstone, the power of the Eternal Moon will be unleashed, and there will be no stopping it."

Elara stared at the cracked stone, her mind racing. The weight of their task pressed down on her like a heavy stone. The prophecy was unfolding faster than any of them had expected, and now the fate of the world rested in their hands.

"How do we fix it?" Elara asked, her voice trembling.

Ilyana's expression hardened with resolve. "There's only one place where the Moonstone can be repaired—at the heart of the Celestial Temple, where the Guardians once held their rituals. It's deep within the mountains, beyond the reach of most mortals."

Dorian let out a low growl. "Of course it is. Why is it never easy?"

Elara swallowed hard, her heart pounding in her chest. They had already come so far, but their journey was far from over. The Moonstone was damaged, the balance of power was shifting, and the Eternal Moon was growing stronger with each passing moment.

But there was no turning back now.

"We'll find the temple," Elara said, her voice steady. "And we'll restore the Moonstone."

Ilyana nodded, her eyes filled with a mixture of fear and determination. "We have no other choice."

As they turned to leave the cavern, the cracked Moonstone safely tucked away in Ilyana's satchel, Elara couldn't shake the feeling that their greatest challenges were still ahead. The illusions and traps they had faced in the cavern were nothing compared to the power they would have to confront when they reached the Celestial Temple.

And as the shadows of the mountain loomed over them, Elara knew that the prophecy was no longer a distant threat.

The Eternal Moon was coming.

And they were running out of time.

Chapter 5: The Curse of the Wolf God

The forest was unnervingly quiet.

Elara's footsteps seemed to echo against the stillness, her senses heightened by the thick, oppressive air that surrounded her and her companions as they made their way deeper into the cursed forest. The trees here were tall and gnarled, their twisted branches reaching toward the sky like skeletal fingers. The underbrush was dense, and the path they had been following for hours had long since disappeared, leaving them to navigate by instinct alone.

Ilyana, who walked just ahead of Elara, paused and looked around warily. "We must be careful. The curse of Fenros is not just a story."

Dorian, the warrior who had joined them on their quest, grunted in agreement but didn't slow his pace. He walked with one hand on the hilt of his sword, his eyes constantly scanning the trees for signs of movement.

Elara could feel the tension between them all. They had entered this forest knowing it was cursed, knowing that the Wolf God Fenros had laid his claim to this land centuries ago. It was said that Fenros, once a powerful deity of the hunt and the moon, had been banished from the world of men when the gods withdrew their presence from the mortal realm. But Fenros had not left willingly. Instead, he had cursed the land with his lingering power, turning it into a place where time twisted and those who stayed too long were transformed into wolves, forever bound to his will.

Now, with the Eternal Moon rising, Elara and her companions knew that Fenros was stirring once more, waiting for his chance to return to full strength. The deeper they ventured into the forest, the more Elara could feel the presence of the Wolf God—an invisible weight pressing down on them, watching their every move.

"How far do you think it is to the center of the forest?" Elara asked, her voice barely above a whisper.

"I don't know," Ilyana replied, glancing at the sky through the tangled branches above. "But we need to hurry. The longer we stay here, the more dangerous it becomes."

Elara nodded, though she couldn't shake the feeling that it was already too late. The air felt thick with magic, the kind that clung to your skin and seeped into your bones. It was as if the forest itself was alive, watching them, waiting for the right moment to strike.

"We should keep moving," Dorian said gruffly, his eyes narrowed as he surveyed the path ahead. "The sooner we get out of this cursed place, the better."

Elara agreed, though her heart was pounding with the knowledge that they couldn't leave until they had faced Fenros. According to the legends, the Wolf God had been waiting for the Night of the Eternal Moon to regain his full power, and now that time was fast approaching. If they didn't confront him soon, there was no telling what havoc he would unleash on the world.

They continued deeper into the forest, the silence growing heavier with each step. The wind, which had once stirred the leaves and rustled the branches, had stilled completely. Even the birds and insects that normally filled the air with their sounds had disappeared, leaving only the hollow sound of their footsteps on the forest floor.

The curse was strong here. Elara could feel it creeping into her mind, making her thoughts slow and disjointed. She shook her head, trying to clear the fog that seemed to be clouding her senses, but it was no use. The deeper they went, the stronger the curse became.

"Do you feel that?" Dorian asked suddenly, his voice low and tense.

Elara nodded, though she wasn't sure how to describe it. It was as if the forest was pulling at her, trying to drag her deeper into its grasp. Her limbs felt heavy, her mind sluggish. She glanced at Ilyana, who was frowning, her brow furrowed in concentration.

"It's the curse," Ilyana said, her voice tight. "We're being affected by it. If we stay here too long, we'll—"

She didn't finish her sentence, but she didn't need to. They all knew the stories—how travelers who entered this forest never returned, how they were transformed into wolves, bound to serve Fenros for eternity. Elara could feel the weight of the curse pressing down on her, but she refused to give in. They had come too far to turn back now.

"We need to find Fenros," Elara said, her voice steadier than she felt. "Before the curse takes hold."

Dorian grunted in agreement, though Elara could see the strain in his eyes. The curse was affecting him too, slowing his movements, clouding his mind. But he pressed on, his hand still firmly on the hilt of his sword.

They walked in silence for what felt like hours, the trees around them growing denser, their twisted branches blocking out what little light remained. The air grew colder, and Elara could feel the weight of the curse growing heavier with each step. Her limbs felt like lead, her thoughts sluggish and disoriented.

Just when Elara thought she couldn't go any farther, they reached a clearing in the center of the forest. The trees parted, revealing a large stone altar in the center of the clearing, its surface cracked and weathered with age. The air around it seemed to hum with energy, a dark, twisted magic that made Elara's skin crawl.

And there, standing beside the altar, was Fenros.

He was not what Elara had expected. The Wolf God was tall, his body lean and muscular, covered in silver fur that shimmered in the faint light. His face was that of a wolf, his eyes glowing a bright, unnatural yellow. He wore no armor, but his presence alone was enough to make Elara's heart race with fear.

"Who dares to enter my domain?" Fenros growled, his voice low and guttural, echoing through the clearing.

Elara stepped forward, her heart pounding in her chest. "We seek an audience with you, Fenros," she said, her voice trembling slightly but steady. "We have come to lift the curse you placed on this forest."

Fenros let out a low, rumbling laugh, his sharp teeth gleaming in the dim light. "You think you can lift my curse? Foolish mortal. This land belongs to me, as do all who enter it."

"We don't seek to challenge your claim," Elara said quickly, her mind racing. "But the Night of the Eternal Moon is coming, and with it, great destruction. If we don't act now, the balance between the mortal and divine realms will be shattered."

Fenros tilted his head, his glowing eyes narrowing as he studied her. "And why should I care about the balance? The gods abandoned this world long ago, leaving us to fend for ourselves. I have waited centuries for the Night of the Eternal Moon to return, so that I may reclaim what is rightfully mine."

Elara swallowed hard, her heart pounding in her chest. "If the balance is destroyed, there will be nothing left for you to reclaim. The world will fall into chaos, and even you won't be able to control it."

For a moment, Fenros was silent, his glowing eyes fixed on her. Elara could feel the weight of his gaze, the power that radiated from him. But she stood her ground, refusing to back down.

Finally, Fenros let out a low growl. "You speak truth, mortal. But what do you propose? I will not lift my curse without something in return."

Elara hesitated, her mind racing. What could she offer a god? She had nothing of value, nothing that could compare to the power of the Eternal Moon. But then, an idea came to her, one that made her heart race with fear and uncertainty.

"I will return after the Eternal Moon has passed," Elara said, her voice steady. "Once the balance has been restored, I will come back and help you regain your place among the gods."

Fenros raised an eyebrow, his glowing eyes narrowing. "And how do I know you will keep your word?"

Elara took a deep breath, her heart pounding in her chest. "Because if I don't, the world will fall into chaos, and we will all be lost. I promise you, Fenros—I will return."

For a long moment, Fenros said nothing, his glowing eyes fixed on her. Elara could feel the weight of his power pressing down on her, testing her resolve. But she stood her ground, refusing to back down.

Finally, Fenros let out a low growl. "Very well, mortal. I will lift the curse—for now. But know this: if you do not return as promised, I will reclaim this land, and all who enter it will belong to me."

Elara nodded, her heart pounding in her chest. "I understand."

Fenros stepped back from the altar, his glowing eyes still fixed on her. "The curse is lifted. But the Night of the Eternal Moon is fast approaching. You must act quickly if you hope to stop it."

With that, Fenros turned and disappeared into the shadows, leaving Elara and her companions standing in the clearing, the weight of the curse finally lifted from their minds.

Elara let out a breath she hadn't realized she'd been holding, her body trembling with relief. They had done it. They had lifted the curse.

But as she looked at the stone altar, its surface cracked and weathered, she couldn't shake the feeling that their journey was far from over. The Night of the Eternal Moon was coming, and with it, the fate of the world hung in the balance.

"We need to move quickly," Ilyana said, her voice tense. "Fenros may have lifted the curse, but the Eternal Moon is still coming. We don't have much time."

Elara nodded, her heart pounding in her chest. The curse had been lifted, but their journey was far from over. The Moonstone was still broken, and the balance between the mortal and divine realms was still at risk.

"We'll return to the Celestial Temple," Elara said, her voice steady. "And we'll fix the Moonstone. Then, when the time comes, I'll return to Fenros."

Dorian grunted in agreement, though Elara could see the strain in his eyes. The curse may have been lifted, but the weight of their journey still hung heavy on them all.

As they turned to leave the clearing, Elara couldn't shake the feeling that the hardest part of their journey was still ahead. The Night of the Eternal Moon was approaching, and with it, the fate of the world rested on their shoulders.

But for now, they had won a small victory. The curse of the Wolf God had been lifted, and the path ahead was clear.

For now.

Chapter 6: The Oracle of the Stars

The wind howled through the jagged peaks of Mount Astralis, carrying with it a chill that seemed to seep into Elara's bones. The sun was setting behind the mountains, casting long shadows over the steep, treacherous path that wound its way up toward the summit. Each step felt heavier than the last, not just because of the thin air at this altitude, but because of the weight of what awaited her at the top.

The Oracle of the Stars—a figure shrouded in mystery, legend, and fear. No one in recent memory had visited the Oracle and returned unchanged. Some said the Oracle's eyes were like twin suns, burning through to your very soul, exposing truths you weren't ready to face. Others claimed that the Oracle spoke only in riddles, leaving you to puzzle over your own fate. But one thing was certain: anyone who sought out the Oracle came seeking answers, and the answers they found were rarely comforting.

Elara had no choice but to go. The curse of the Wolf God had been lifted temporarily, but the Eternal Moon was approaching faster than she had anticipated. The Moonstone was broken, its power unstable, and unless it could be restored, the balance between the mortal and divine realms would collapse, plunging the world into chaos. Ilyana, the wise healer who had guided her through much of her journey, had insisted that only the Oracle could provide the answers they needed to understand Elara's role in the prophecy.

But the Oracle of the Stars was more than just a source of knowledge. According to the legends, the Oracle could see both the past and the future, threading the two together to reveal the truth of one's destiny. Elara feared what she might learn—what hidden truths about herself the Oracle might unveil.

Ahead of her, Ilyana was moving steadily, her movements sure and graceful despite the treacherous terrain. Dorian followed closely behind Elara, his ever-watchful eyes scanning their surroundings for any signs of danger. The thin air at this altitude had left them all quiet, conserving their energy for the long trek ahead, but the silence between them was filled with unspoken thoughts and fears.

Elara's mind raced as she climbed, her thoughts swirling with everything they had been through so far. The curse of the Wolf God, Fenros, had been temporarily lifted, but the danger was far from over. Fenros had warned her that the balance between the mortal and divine realms was fragile, and unless the Moonstone was repaired, the Eternal Moon would bring destruction to both realms. She had promised to return after the Eternal Moon to help restore order, but in truth, she had no idea how she was supposed to fulfill that promise.

And now, as they neared the Oracle's domain, the questions weighed heavier on her. What if she wasn't strong enough? What if she failed?

"Elara," Ilyana's voice called softly from ahead, snapping her out of her thoughts. "We're nearly there."

Elara nodded, though her heart pounded with both fear and anticipation. The path was steep, the wind cutting through her cloak like a knife, but she pushed forward, determined to reach the summit.

The final stretch of the climb was the hardest. The rocks beneath their feet were loose, and every step threatened to send them tumbling back down the mountain. But at last, they reached the summit—a narrow plateau surrounded by jagged cliffs and towering peaks.

At the center of the plateau stood a small stone structure, ancient and weathered by centuries of wind and snow. The building had no roof, only four pillars that supported the remains of what had once been a grand temple. The walls were carved with symbols of the stars, intricate constellations that shimmered faintly in the dying light of the setting sun.

And there, standing in the center of the ruined temple, was the Oracle.

She was tall and slender, her robes flowing around her like the night sky itself. Her hair was long and silver, and her eyes—Elara's breath caught in her throat when she saw them—her eyes were like stars, glowing with an otherworldly light. The Oracle's gaze was fixed on the horizon, as if she were watching something that no one else could see.

Ilyana and Dorian both stopped at the edge of the temple, giving Elara a nod as if to tell her this moment was hers alone. Elara swallowed her fear and stepped forward, her heart pounding in her chest.

"Oracle," Elara said, her voice barely a whisper.

The Oracle turned slowly to face her, and Elara felt the weight of those star-filled eyes settle on her. It was like being laid bare, as if every secret, every fear, every doubt she had ever harbored was exposed in that moment. Elara wanted to look away, but she couldn't.

"Child of the mortal and divine," the Oracle said, her voice soft but filled with power. "You seek answers."

Elara nodded, her throat dry. "I do. I need to know... how to stop the Eternal Moon. How to restore the balance."

The Oracle tilted her head slightly, her glowing eyes narrowing. "The answers you seek lie within you. But you must be willing to face the truth of your lineage. Only then will you understand your place in the prophecy."

Elara frowned. "My lineage? I don't understand."

The Oracle's gaze softened, and she gestured for Elara to come closer. "Come. Let me show you."

Elara hesitated for only a moment before stepping forward. As she did, the Oracle reached out and placed her hand on Elara's forehead. Instantly, the world around her seemed to dissolve, and Elara felt herself being pulled into a vision.

She stood in a vast, endless void, surrounded by stars. The sky above her was a swirling tapestry of constellations, each one glowing with a soft, ethereal light. Elara looked around, but there was no one else—just the stars and the infinite darkness.

Then, from the void, a figure appeared—a woman, tall and radiant, with silver hair that flowed like water and eyes that glowed like the sun. She wore a crown of stars, and her presence was so powerful that Elara felt herself tremble in awe.

"Who are you?" Elara asked, her voice barely audible in the vastness of the void.

The woman smiled, and the stars around her seemed to pulse with light. "I am Selene, the goddess of the moon and the night. And I am your ancestor."

Elara's breath caught in her throat. "My ancestor?"

Selene nodded, her expression softening. "You are of my blood, Elara. You carry the legacy of the gods within you. That is why you have been chosen."

Elara's mind raced. Her ancestor? She had always known there was something different about her, something that set her apart from others, but she had never imagined that her lineage was tied to the gods themselves.

"What does this mean?" Elara asked, her voice trembling. "Why was I chosen?"

"Because you are the key to restoring the balance between the mortal and divine realms," Selene said, her voice filled with both sorrow and hope. "The bond between our realms has been broken for centuries, ever since the gods withdrew from the world of men. The Eternal Moon is the final reckoning—if the balance is not restored, the mortal realm will fall into eternal darkness."

Elara swallowed hard, her heart pounding in her chest. "But how? How can I restore the balance?"

"You must repair the Moonstone," Selene said. "It is the conduit through which the power of the Eternal Moon flows. If the Moonstone remains broken, the power will be unleashed, and the world will fall into chaos."

Elara nodded, though her mind was still reeling from the revelation of her divine ancestry. "I understand. But... why me? Why was I chosen?"

Selene's gaze softened, and she stepped closer to Elara, placing a gentle hand on her shoulder. "Because you have the strength to bridge the gap between our realms. You are both mortal and divine, and only one with your lineage can restore the broken bond."

Elara felt tears prick at her eyes. The weight of her responsibility was overwhelming, but there was also a sense of clarity that she hadn't felt before. She had been searching for answers, and now she understood—she was the key to stopping the Eternal Moon, the bridge between the mortal and divine realms.

"But what if I fail?" Elara whispered, her voice trembling. "What if I'm not strong enough?"

Selene smiled gently. "You are stronger than you know, Elara. The power of the gods flows within you, but it is your heart, your courage, and your determination that will guide you."

The void around them began to shimmer, and Elara felt herself being pulled back to reality. "Remember," Selene said, her voice growing distant, "the future is not set in stone. You have the power to shape it."

ELARA GASPED AS SHE was pulled out of the vision, her knees buckling beneath her. She stumbled, but the Oracle caught her, steadying her with a firm hand.

"You have seen the truth," the Oracle said, her voice soft. "Now you understand."

Elara nodded, her heart pounding in her chest. "I'm... I'm descended from the gods."

"Yes," the Oracle replied. "And that is why the prophecy revolves around you. You alone can restore the broken bond between the realms."

Elara took a deep breath, trying to steady herself. The weight of her lineage, of the responsibility that had been placed on her shoulders, was almost too much to bear. But she couldn't allow herself to falter. The fate of the world depended on her.

"The Moonstone," Elara said, her voice steadying. "I need to repair it. How do I do that?"

The Oracle's glowing eyes seemed to pierce through her, and for a moment, Elara felt as though the Oracle could see into every corner of her soul. "The Moonstone is not just an object of power—it is a symbol of the bond between the mortal and divine realms. To repair it, you must restore that bond."

"How?" Elara asked, her voice tinged with desperation.

"You must forge a new connection between the realms," the Oracle said. "A bond built not on domination, but on cooperation and understanding. The gods will not simply return to the world of men, nor should they. But the balance must be restored, or both realms will fall."

Elara nodded, though her heart pounded with fear. The task before her was daunting, but she had no choice. She had to succeed.

"And what happens if I fail?" Elara asked, her voice barely above a whisper.

The Oracle's gaze darkened, and for the first time, Elara saw a flicker of sadness in her glowing eyes. "If you fail, the Eternal Moon will unleash its full power, plunging the world into eternal darkness. The mortal realm will be consumed, and the gods will be forever lost to us."

Elara's breath caught in her throat. Eternal darkness. The end of everything. She couldn't let that happen.

"I won't fail," Elara said, her voice filled with determination. "I can't."

The Oracle nodded, though her expression remained solemn. "Remember, child of the stars, the future is not set in stone. You have the power to shape it, but the path will not be easy."

Elara took a deep breath, her mind racing with everything she had learned. Her journey was far from over, but now, she understood her role in the prophecy. She was the bridge between the mortal and divine realms, and it was up to her to restore the balance before the Eternal Moon brought destruction to the world.

"I'm ready," Elara said, her voice steady. "I'll do whatever it takes."

The Oracle smiled faintly, her glowing eyes softening. "Then go, Elara. Your destiny awaits."

With that, Elara turned and left the ruined temple, her heart filled with both fear and hope. The future was uncertain, and the path ahead was fraught with danger, but she was no longer the same person who had set out on this journey. She was descended from the gods, and she had the power to shape the fate of the world.

But as she descended the mountain with Ilyana and Dorian by her side, the weight of the Oracle's words lingered in her mind.

The future was not set in stone.

And failure was not an option.

Chapter 7: The Realm of Forgotten Gods

The journey into the Realm of Forgotten Gods began with a quiet, unnatural stillness. The air itself seemed heavy, thick with an energy that Elara had never felt before. It weighed on her chest, making it hard to breathe, as though the very atmosphere of this place was trying to push them back, to reject their presence.

They had left the familiar world behind, stepping through the portal that Ilyana had found buried in an ancient text. It was said that this was the only way to reach the forgotten gods—those deities who had once ruled the heavens, but had since been cast into this shadowy dimension, where their power had waned and their memories faded from the minds of mortals.

Elara could feel the change immediately. The colors around her seemed duller, the sounds muted, as if they were walking through a world stuck between existence and oblivion. The sky, if it could even be called that, was a strange, swirling gray, neither day nor night, and the ground beneath their feet was soft, almost spongy, as if they were walking on the remnants of something long dead.

Dorian, ever vigilant, walked beside her, his hand resting on the hilt of his sword. He had grown more quiet as they entered this strange place, his sharp eyes scanning their surroundings for any sign of danger. Ilyana led the way, her face calm but her body tense, every step measured and careful.

"This place... it feels wrong," Elara whispered, glancing around at the strange landscape. Trees with twisted, skeletal branches rose from the ground, their bark blackened and cracked as if they had been scorched by some ancient fire. The air was cold, but there was no wind, and the silence was so complete that it felt oppressive.

"It is wrong," Ilyana replied quietly, not turning around. "This is a realm of gods who have been forgotten, abandoned by mortals and banished from the divine realm. Their power has faded, but they still exist... in a twisted, broken form."

Elara shivered, not from the cold, but from the knowledge of where they were. The forgotten gods were the ones who had been left behind when the mortal and divine realms had split. While the major gods had retreated to their own domain, leaving the world of mortals to govern itself, the lesser, forgotten gods had been cast aside, their influence fading as mortals stopped worshipping them. Now, they were little more than shadows of their former selves, trapped in this realm of despair and madness.

"We need to find Selene," Elara said, her voice steadier than she felt. "She's the only one who can help us repair the Moonstone."

Ilyana nodded. "Yes, but finding her won't be easy. The gods here... they've lost much of themselves. Some have descended into madness. Others are filled with anger and bitterness. We must be careful not to provoke them."

Dorian grunted in agreement, his eyes narrowing as he scanned the twisted trees and jagged rocks around them. "I don't like this place. It feels like we're being watched."

Elara felt it too. There was a presence in the air, something just out of sight, lurking in the shadows. She couldn't shake the feeling that they were not alone, that the forgotten gods were watching them, waiting to see what they would do.

As they moved deeper into the realm, the landscape grew more twisted and surreal. The ground shifted beneath their feet, sometimes hard as stone, other times soft as sand. The trees became more distorted, their branches curling inward like claws, and strange, flickering lights danced in the distance, casting eerie shadows across the ground.

They had been walking for hours, though it was impossible to tell time in this place. There was no sun, no stars, only the endless gray sky above them. The silence was overwhelming, broken only by the sound of their footsteps and the occasional rustle of something moving just out of sight.

Finally, they reached what appeared to be a ruined temple, its walls cracked and crumbling, covered in vines that seemed to writhe and twist like living creatures. The entrance was dark, a gaping hole that seemed to lead into the very heart of the mountain. Elara's heart pounded in her chest as they approached, but she knew this was where they had to go.

"This must be it," Ilyana said, her voice low. "The temple of Selene."

Elara stared at the entrance, her mind racing with the stories she had heard about the moon goddess. Selene had once been a powerful deity, the goddess of the moon and the night, revered by mortals for her beauty and wisdom. But as the gods withdrew from the mortal realm, Selene had been forgotten, her temples abandoned, her name lost to time. Now, she was one of the forgotten gods, trapped in this shadowy realm, her power diminished but not entirely gone.

"Do you think she'll help us?" Elara asked, her voice trembling slightly. "If we can even find her?"

Ilyana's expression was unreadable. "That depends on whether she still remembers what it means to care about the mortal world."

Elara took a deep breath and stepped forward, crossing the threshold of the ruined temple. The air inside was colder, thicker, and as she walked deeper into the darkness, she felt the weight of the place pressing down on her. It was as if the temple itself was alive, watching her, judging her.

The temple's interior was vast, with high ceilings that disappeared into shadow. The walls were lined with ancient carvings, depicting scenes of the moon and the night sky, but they were faded and worn, barely visible in the dim light. Elara could feel the power in this place, though it was faint, like the last flicker of a dying flame.

As they walked through the temple, they came to a large chamber, its floor cracked and uneven, with a massive stone throne at the far end. Sitting on the throne was a figure—a woman, tall and slender, her hair long and silver, her skin pale as moonlight. Her eyes were closed, and her head rested against the back of the throne, as if she were asleep. But even in her slumber, there was an aura of power around her, a presence that filled the room.

"Selene," Elara whispered, her heart racing. This was the goddess they had been searching for.

Ilyana stepped forward cautiously. "Be careful. She may not be the goddess you expect."

As if in response to Ilyana's words, Selene's eyes slowly opened. They were like twin moons, glowing with a soft, silver light. She blinked once, twice, as if waking from a long dream, and then her gaze settled on Elara.

"Who dares enter my domain?" Selene's voice was soft, but there was a sharpness to it, a cold edge that sent a shiver down Elara's spine.

Elara took a deep breath and stepped forward, her hands trembling slightly. "My name is Elara. I've come to ask for your help."

Selene's gaze flickered over her, then shifted to Ilyana and Dorian. "Help? You come seeking the aid of a forgotten goddess? A goddess who has been cast aside by mortals, abandoned and left to fade into nothingness?"

Elara swallowed hard. "We haven't forgotten you. I haven't forgotten you. That's why I'm here."

Selene's lips curled into a faint, bitter smile. "You say that now, but where were you when my temples were abandoned? When my name was erased from the minds of men? You mortals are fickle creatures, quick to forget those who once held power over you."

Elara could feel the weight of Selene's anger, but she didn't back down. "I know that the gods have been forgotten, but I haven't come to ask for forgiveness. I've come because the balance between the mortal and divine realms is in danger. The Eternal Moon is coming, and if we don't stop it, both realms will be destroyed."

Selene's eyes narrowed, her gaze sharp and piercing. "The Eternal Moon... So, the prophecy is coming to pass."

Elara nodded. "Yes. And I need your help to stop it."

For a long moment, Selene was silent, her eyes flickering with something Elara couldn't quite place—regret, anger, sorrow? The goddess leaned back in her throne, her gaze distant as if she were remembering something long buried in the past.

"I once cared for the mortal realm," Selene said softly, her voice tinged with bitterness. "I watched over the night, guiding those who wandered in darkness. But when the gods withdrew, I was cast aside. Mortals forgot me. My temples crumbled, and my name was lost to time."

Elara's heart ached at the sadness in Selene's voice. "But you're still here. You still have power."

Selene's gaze shifted back to Elara, her eyes cold and unreadable. "What do you ask of me, mortal?"

Elara swallowed hard. "The Moonstone is broken. I need your power to repair it, to restore the balance between the realms. Without it, the Eternal Moon will bring eternal darkness."

Selene was silent for a long time, her eyes studying Elara with an intensity that made her feel as if the goddess could see straight through her. Finally, Selene rose from her throne, her movements graceful and fluid, like a shadow gliding across the floor.

"You speak of restoring balance, but do you understand what that means?" Selene asked, her voice soft but filled with an ancient wisdom. "To restore the balance between the mortal and divine

realms is not simply a matter of repairing a broken stone. It is a matter of rekindling the bond between our worlds. A bond that has been severed for centuries."

Elara nodded, her heart pounding in her chest. "I understand. And I'm willing to do whatever it takes to restore that bond."

Selene's gaze softened slightly, and for the first time, Elara saw a flicker of hope in the goddess's eyes. "You carry the blood of the gods, Elara. You are not like the mortals who abandoned us. You have the power to bridge the gap between our worlds."

Elara's breath caught in her throat. "You... you know about my lineage?"

Selene nodded. "Yes. I can feel it in you—the blood of the divine flows through your veins. That is why you were chosen."

Elara took a deep breath, her mind racing with the weight of her responsibility. "Then will you help me?"

Selene was silent for a moment, her eyes flickering with uncertainty. "I will help you, Elara. But know this—the path ahead will not be easy. The other gods... they are not like me. They have fallen into madness and despair, consumed by their anger and bitterness. They will not aid you willingly."

Elara nodded, her heart pounding in her chest. "I understand. But I have to try."

Selene smiled faintly, her glowing eyes softening. "Then I will give you what power I have left. But be warned—the balance between our realms is fragile. If you fail, the Eternal Moon will bring eternal darkness, and both the mortal and divine realms will be lost."

Elara swallowed hard, her heart pounding with fear and determination. "I won't fail."

With that, Selene raised her hand, and a soft, silver light enveloped Elara. She could feel the goddess's power flowing through her, filling her with strength and clarity. The weight of the journey ahead still hung heavy on her shoulders, but for the first time, she felt a glimmer of hope.

As the light faded, Selene stepped back, her eyes once again distant and unreadable. "Go, Elara. The fate of the world rests in your hands."

Elara nodded, her heart filled with both fear and hope. She turned and left the temple, Ilyana and Dorian following close behind. The journey ahead was fraught with danger, but now, with Selene's power guiding her, she knew that she had a chance to restore the balance and stop the Eternal Moon.

But as they left the Realm of Forgotten Gods, Elara couldn't shake the feeling that the hardest part of their journey was still ahead. The forgotten gods were not all as willing as Selene, and the power of the Eternal Moon was growing stronger with each passing day.

The fate of both realms rested on her shoulders.

And failure was not an option.

Chapter 8: The Betrayal of Dorian

The mountain air was cold, the sharpness of it biting against Elara's skin as she and her companions descended from the Realm of Forgotten Gods. Their victory in gaining Selene's aid should have filled her with hope, but instead, a growing sense of unease weighed on her heart. The journey had grown increasingly dangerous, and the looming threat of the Eternal Moon felt closer than ever. Every step they took felt like they were marching toward the edge of a precipice, one that could plunge them into eternal darkness.

Elara glanced at Dorian, the warrior who had been by her side from the beginning. His expression was unreadable, his jaw clenched, and his eyes set firmly ahead. He had always been stoic, but in the past few days, something had changed. He had become more withdrawn, more guarded. Every time their eyes met, there was something in his gaze—something dark and uncertain.

She couldn't shake the feeling that something was wrong.

Ilyana, walking a few paces ahead, seemed to sense it too. The healer had always been perceptive, and though she had not voiced her concerns, Elara could tell that she was keeping a close eye on Dorian as well. The trust that had once bound them together was beginning to unravel, frayed by secrets and doubts that none of them dared to speak aloud.

As they made camp that night, the tension between them became even more palpable. They sat around the fire in silence, the crackling flames doing little to dispel the cold that seemed to seep into their bones. The stars above were obscured by clouds, and the only sound was the distant howling of wind through the mountains.

Elara poked at the fire with a stick, her mind racing. She knew they were running out of time. The Eternal Moon was fast approaching, and they still had much to do. But the weight of their task wasn't the only thing pressing on her. There was something else—something deeper, more personal.

Dorian's betrayal.

Though he hadn't yet acted on it, Elara had seen the signs. The way he avoided her gaze, the way his hand lingered near his sword whenever they spoke of the Moonstone, and the way he had begun to question their mission at every turn. She had tried to push the doubts aside, to tell herself that Dorian was just being cautious, that the pressure of their journey was weighing on him as it was on all of them.

But the truth was harder to ignore.

Elara glanced across the fire at Dorian, who was sharpening his blade with slow, deliberate movements. His face was shadowed by the firelight, but there was no mistaking the tension in his posture. He hadn't said a word since they had made camp, and the silence between them felt like a chasm.

Finally, Elara couldn't stand it any longer.

"Dorian," she said quietly, her voice barely carrying over the crackling of the fire. "We need to talk."

Dorian didn't look up from his blade, but his jaw tightened. "About what?"

"You know what," Elara replied, her voice steady despite the pounding of her heart. "Something's been bothering you. I can see it. I've seen it for days now."

Ilyana shifted slightly, her gaze flicking between the two of them. She didn't speak, but the tension in her posture showed that she was ready for whatever might happen next.

Dorian finally looked up, his eyes meeting Elara's. For a moment, he said nothing, but there was a storm brewing behind his gaze—something dark and dangerous that Elara had never seen before.

"Bothering me?" Dorian repeated, his voice low and bitter. "You want to know what's bothering me?"

Elara nodded, her heart pounding in her chest. "Yes. I want to know."

Dorian stood up suddenly, his movements sharp and tense. He sheathed his blade with a snap and began pacing around the fire, his eyes never leaving Elara's. "What's bothering me, Elara, is that we've been running around chasing relics, fighting gods, and trying to stop this prophecy from coming true, and for what? To restore some ancient balance between mortals and gods? Do you really think that's going to solve anything?"

Elara frowned, her confusion growing. "What are you talking about? The balance between the mortal and divine realms is breaking. If we don't repair the Moonstone, the Eternal Moon will destroy everything."

Dorian laughed, but there was no humor in it. "Destroy everything? Or finally free us from the gods' control?"

Elara's breath caught in her throat. "What are you saying?"

Dorian stopped pacing and turned to face her, his eyes blazing with anger and something else—something darker. "I'm saying that maybe the Eternal Moon isn't the end of the world. Maybe it's the beginning of something new. Maybe it's time we stopped bowing to the gods and let the world belong to mortals again."

Elara's heart pounded in her chest. "That's madness, Dorian. If the Eternal Moon comes, it will plunge the world into eternal darkness. It's not about freeing mortals from the gods—it's about survival."

"Survival?" Dorian spat, his voice rising. "Or submission? You talk about restoring balance, but all you're doing is playing into the gods' hands. They don't care about us, Elara. They never have. They abandoned us long ago, and now you want to restore their power?"

Elara stood, her fists clenched at her sides. "That's not what this is about, and you know it. The gods may have left, but their power still affects our world. If we don't restore the balance, everything will be destroyed."

Dorian took a step closer, his face inches from hers. "You don't understand, Elara. There's more at stake here than you realize."

Elara's heart raced as she stared into his eyes, searching for any sign of the man she had once trusted. "What do you mean?"

Dorian hesitated for a moment, and then the words tumbled out of him, as if he had been holding them back for too long. "One of the old gods came to me. They promised me power—more power than you can imagine—if I hand over the Moonstone."

Elara's blood ran cold. "What?"

Dorian's eyes darkened. "I could have everything, Elara. Power, immortality... the old gods are offering us a chance to change the world, to take control of our own destiny. And you want to throw that away? For what? To keep things the way they've always been?"

Elara's mind raced. She had trusted Dorian. He had been by her side from the beginning, had fought alongside her, had protected her. And now, he was talking about betraying her, about handing over the Moonstone to one of the very gods they had been fighting against.

"Dorian," she whispered, her voice trembling. "You can't be serious."

Dorian took another step closer, his eyes burning with intensity. "I'm dead serious, Elara. This is our chance—my chance—to finally take control of our lives, to break free from the gods' influence. And I'm not going to let you throw it all away."

Elara's heart pounded in her chest as she stared at him, her mind spinning. She couldn't believe what she was hearing. The Dorian she knew—the man who had fought by her side, who had protected her—was gone. In his place stood someone she barely recognized, someone who was willing to betray everything they had fought for.

"I can't let you do this," Elara said, her voice steady despite the fear that gripped her heart.

Dorian's eyes narrowed. "And what are you going to do about it? Stop me?"

Elara's hand moved to the hilt of her sword, but she hesitated. She didn't want to fight him. Not after everything they had been through together. "Dorian, please. Think about what you're doing. The old gods don't care about you. They're using you."

Dorian's expression twisted into a sneer. "And you think the gods you're trying to protect are any different? They're all the same, Elara. They take what they want and leave us to pick up the pieces."

Elara's heart ached as she looked at him. "But that's not who you are. You're better than this."

For a moment, Dorian's expression faltered, and Elara saw a flicker of doubt in his eyes. But it was gone as quickly as it had appeared, replaced by cold determination.

"No," Dorian said, his voice hard. "I've made my choice."

Before Elara could react, Dorian lunged at her, his sword drawn. The movement was quick, fluid, and deadly, and Elara barely had time to raise her own blade to block the attack. The sound of steel clashing against steel echoed through the night as they circled each other, their swords flashing in the firelight.

"Dorian, stop!" Elara cried, her heart pounding in her chest. "You don't have to do this!"

But Dorian's face was twisted with rage, his eyes filled with a burning intensity that sent a chill down Elara's spine. "You're too blind to see it, Elara! The gods are playing us all!"

Their swords clashed again, the force of the impact reverberating through Elara's arms. She could see the strain in Dorian's movements, the desperation in his eyes. He was fighting not just against her, but against something inside himself.

"Dorian, please," Elara pleaded, her voice breaking. "You're better than this. Don't let them control you."

For a moment, Dorian hesitated, his sword lowering slightly as if her words had reached him. But then his expression hardened once more, and he swung his blade with renewed force. Elara blocked the strike, her muscles burning with the effort.

"I won't let you stop me," Dorian snarled, his voice filled with anger and pain.

Elara's heart ached as she fought him, every movement heavy with the knowledge that this was not the man she had known. Dorian had been consumed by his desire for power, blinded by the promise of something greater than himself. But beneath that anger, Elara could still see the man she had once trusted, the man who had fought by her side.

With a final, desperate surge of strength, Elara disarmed Dorian, sending his sword flying from his hand. He stumbled back, breathing heavily, his eyes wide with shock and anger.

"Dorian," Elara said, her voice soft but firm. "It's over."

For a long moment, Dorian stood there, his chest heaving, his fists clenched at his sides. Then, slowly, the fight seemed to drain out of him. His shoulders sagged, and the fire in his eyes dimmed.

"I... I made a mistake," Dorian whispered, his voice trembling with regret. "I thought... I thought I could change everything. I thought I could make things better."

Elara's heart ached as she looked at him. "You can still make things right, Dorian. You don't have to do this."

Dorian's gaze flickered toward the fire, and for a moment, Elara thought he might listen. But then his expression hardened once more, and he shook his head.

"No," Dorian said quietly. "It's too late for me."

Before Elara could stop him, Dorian lunged toward the fire, grabbing the Moonstone from where it lay beside Ilyana's pack. Elara's heart leaped into her throat as she realized what he was about to do.

"Dorian, no!"

But it was too late. With a look of grim determination, Dorian held the Moonstone above his head and then brought it down with all his strength, shattering it against the rocks.

The sound of the Moonstone breaking echoed through the night, a sharp, piercing crack that seemed to reverberate through the very air around them. Elara felt the power of the stone shatter like glass, its energy spilling out into the world, uncontrolled and wild.

Dorian collapsed to the ground, his face pale, his body trembling. Elara rushed to his side, her heart pounding with fear and grief.

"Why did you do it?" she whispered, her voice breaking.

Dorian looked up at her, his eyes filled with pain and regret. "I thought... I thought it was the only way."

Elara shook her head, tears streaming down her face. "You didn't have to do this. We could have stopped it."

Dorian smiled weakly, his breath shallow. "I'm sorry, Elara. I'm so sorry."

And with those final words, Dorian's body went still, his eyes closing as the life left him.

Elara knelt beside him, her heart shattered. The Moonstone was broken, and the man she had trusted had betrayed her. The unity of their group was fractured, and the future had never seemed so uncertain.

But as Elara looked down at Dorian's lifeless body, she knew one thing for certain—the fight was far from over.

Chapter 9: The Eternal Moon Rises

The world seemed to hold its breath as the first sliver of the Eternal Moon rose into the night sky. It was unlike any other moon Elara had ever seen—larger, brighter, and more luminous than the moon that mortals were accustomed to. Its pale silver light bathed the land in an eerie glow, casting long shadows that twisted and writhed as if alive. The sky, once filled with stars, was now a swirling canvas of silvery mist, and the air itself seemed to shimmer with strange magic.

Elara stood at the edge of a cliff, gazing up at the sky, her heart heavy with the weight of the prophecy. This was the moment she had been dreading, the moment that had haunted her dreams ever since she had learned of her role in the prophecy. The Eternal Moon was rising, and with it, the world was changing.

Beside her, Ilyana stood silent, her expression calm but tense. The healer had always been a steady presence, her wisdom and guidance invaluable throughout their journey. But now, even Ilyana seemed to sense the gravity of the situation. The air was thick with anticipation, as if the very fabric of reality was beginning to unravel.

"Do you feel it?" Elara whispered, her voice barely audible over the wind that whipped through her hair.

Ilyana nodded, her eyes fixed on the moon. "Yes. The magic is stronger now. It's as if the boundaries between our world and the realm of the gods are thinning."

Elara swallowed hard, her heart pounding in her chest. "We don't have much time, do we?"

"No," Ilyana replied, her voice soft but firm. "The Eternal Moon has begun its ascent. If we don't reach the Temple of the Moon before it reaches its zenith, all will be lost."

Elara felt a surge of panic rise within her, but she forced herself to remain calm. They had come too far to falter now. Dorian's betrayal had shaken her to her core, but she couldn't let that stop her. The Moonstone had been shattered, but there was still hope. Selene, the moon goddess, had given her the knowledge she needed to perform the ritual. If they could reach the temple in time, they could still save the world.

But the path ahead was fraught with danger. The Eternal Moon's rise had awakened forces that had long been dormant—creatures of myth and legend that had once walked the earth but had since faded into obscurity. Elara could already feel their presence, lurking at the edges of her awareness. The world was shifting, bending to the will of the Eternal Moon, and nothing would ever be the same.

"We should go," Elara said, turning away from the cliff. "We need to reach the temple before it's too late."

Ilyana nodded in agreement and began gathering her things. The wind howled around them as they packed up their camp, the silvery light of the Eternal Moon casting strange, flickering shadows across the ground. Elara's heart pounded with urgency as she strapped her sword to her side and slung her pack over her shoulder.

As they set off, the path ahead was difficult to navigate. The land itself seemed to have been altered by the rising of the Eternal Moon. The ground was uneven, and the air was thick with magic, making it hard to breathe. Strange, flickering lights appeared in the distance, and Elara could hear the faint sounds of creatures moving through the darkness. Every rustle of leaves, every snap of a branch, made her skin prickle with unease.

They moved quickly, but the journey felt longer than it should have. The Temple of the Moon was located deep within a forest, hidden from view by towering trees and dense underbrush. According to the legends, the temple had been built by the first worshippers of Selene, a place where the goddess could commune with mortals during times of great need. Now, it was their only hope of stopping the Eternal Moon from plunging the world into chaos.

As they walked, Elara's thoughts drifted to Dorian. His betrayal had left a deep wound, one that would take time to heal. She had trusted him, relied on him, and in the end, he had chosen power over loyalty. But even in his final moments, he had shown remorse. He had tried to make things right, sacrificing himself to protect her and Ilyana from the consequences of his actions. It was a bitter consolation, but it was all she had.

"He made his choice," Ilyana said quietly, as if reading Elara's thoughts. "And in the end, he tried to atone for it."

Elara nodded, though the pain of his betrayal still lingered. "I know. But it doesn't make it any easier."

"No," Ilyana agreed, her voice soft. "It never does."

They walked in silence for a while longer, the only sound the crunch of leaves beneath their boots and the distant rustling of the forest. Elara kept her hand on the hilt of her sword, her senses alert to any potential danger. The magic in the air was thick, and she knew that the creatures of the Eternal Moon would not hesitate to attack if given the chance.

As they neared the edge of the forest, the trees grew taller, their branches arching overhead like a cathedral of wood and shadow. The light of the Eternal Moon filtered through the leaves, casting strange, shifting patterns on the ground. Elara's heart raced as they entered the forest, the path ahead barely visible in the dim light.

"We're getting close," Ilyana said, her voice tense. "The temple should be just ahead."

Elara nodded, though her nerves were on edge. The air here felt different—heavier, more charged with magic. She could feel the presence of something ancient and powerful, something that had been waiting for this moment for centuries.

They pushed forward, the trees closing in around them, the path becoming more difficult to navigate. The underbrush was thick, and every step felt like a struggle. But Elara knew they couldn't afford to slow down. Time was running out, and the Eternal Moon was rising higher in the sky with every passing moment.

Suddenly, a sound reached her ears—a low, guttural growl that sent a shiver down her spine. Elara froze, her hand tightening on the hilt of her sword. The growl came again, closer this time, followed by the sound of heavy footsteps moving through the trees.

"Something's coming," Elara whispered, her voice barely audible.

Ilyana's eyes darted around the forest, her hand moving to the pouch at her waist where she kept her healing herbs. "Be ready."

Elara drew her sword, the blade gleaming in the silver light of the Eternal Moon. The growling grew louder, and Elara could hear the sound of branches snapping as something large moved toward them. Her heart pounded in her chest as she strained her eyes, trying to catch a glimpse of whatever creature was stalking them.

Then, from the shadows of the trees, a massive figure emerged.

It was a creature out of legend—a giant wolf, its fur black as night and its eyes glowing with an unnatural silver light. Its teeth were bared in a snarl, and its massive paws crushed the ground beneath it as it moved closer, circling them with predatory intent.

Elara's breath caught in her throat. The creature was larger than any wolf she had ever seen, its body rippling with muscle and power. This was no ordinary beast—it was one of the creatures of the Eternal Moon, brought back into the world by the magic that now filled the air.

Ilyana took a step back, her eyes wide with fear. "We need to be careful. This is no ordinary wolf."

Elara nodded, her grip on her sword tightening. "I know."

The wolf circled them, its glowing eyes fixed on Elara. She could feel the weight of its gaze, as if it were measuring her, testing her resolve. The air was thick with tension, and for a moment, everything seemed to hang in the balance.

Then, without warning, the wolf lunged.

Elara moved quickly, raising her sword to block the attack. The force of the impact sent a jolt through her arms, but she held her ground, her blade flashing as she deflected the wolf's powerful strikes. The creature was fast—faster than anything she had ever faced—but she was determined not to let it overwhelm her.

Ilyana moved to the side, her hands glowing with magic as she prepared a spell. Elara could feel the energy building around them, the air crackling with power. But the wolf was relentless, its attacks coming faster and harder with each passing moment.

Elara ducked under a swipe of the wolf's massive claws, her heart racing as she tried to find an opening. The creature's glowing eyes never left her, its movements precise and deadly. She knew that one wrong move could mean the end.

Suddenly, the wolf reared back, its jaws open wide as it prepared to strike again. Elara saw her chance. With a swift, fluid movement, she lunged forward, driving her sword into the wolf's side. The creature let out a deafening howl of pain, its massive body shuddering as it stumbled backward.

Ilyana's spell hit the wolf a moment later, a burst of light and energy that sent the creature crashing to the ground. The air was filled with the sound of the wolf's pained growls as it writhed in the dirt, its silver eyes dimming.

Elara stood over the fallen creature, her chest heaving with the effort of the fight. The wolf's body twitched once, twice, and then it went still, its glowing eyes finally closing as it succumbed to its wounds.

For a moment, the forest was silent.

Elara lowered her sword, her heart still racing. "Is it... is it dead?"

Ilyana stepped closer, her eyes narrowing as she examined the creature. "I think so. But we should move quickly. There may be more of them."

Elara nodded, wiping the sweat from her brow. The air was still thick with magic, and she could feel the presence of other creatures lurking in the shadows. The Eternal Moon's rise had awakened forces that had long been dormant, and they would not hesitate to attack again.

"We're close to the temple," Ilyana said, her voice urgent. "We need to keep moving."

Elara sheathed her sword, her muscles aching from the fight. They had no time to rest. The Eternal Moon was rising higher in the sky, and every moment they wasted brought them closer to the point of no return.

They moved quickly through the forest, their footsteps silent as they navigated the dense underbrush. The trees loomed overhead, their branches twisted and gnarled, and the air was filled with the strange, otherworldly light of the Eternal Moon.

Finally, after what felt like hours, they reached the edge of the forest.

Before them, nestled in a clearing surrounded by towering trees, stood the Temple of the Moon.

The temple was ancient, its stone walls covered in moss and vines, its entrance flanked by towering statues of the moon goddess, Selene. The silver light of the Eternal Moon bathed the temple in an ethereal glow, casting long shadows that danced across the ground.

Elara's heart pounded as she gazed up at the temple. This was it. The place where the ritual would be performed. The place where the fate of the world would be decided.

Ilyana stepped forward, her eyes wide with awe. "We made it."

Elara nodded, though her mind was already racing with the task ahead. The ritual was complex, and there was no room for error. If they failed, the Eternal Moon would plunge the world into eternal darkness, and all would be lost.

"We need to hurry," Elara said, her voice steady. "The moon is almost at its zenith."

Ilyana nodded in agreement, and together they approached the temple.

The entrance was dark and foreboding, the air inside thick with the weight of centuries of magic. Elara could feel the power of the place, the ancient energy that had been woven into the very stones of the temple. This was where the first worshippers of Selene had performed their rituals, where the bond between the mortal and divine realms had once been strongest.

Now, it was their only hope.

They entered the temple, their footsteps echoing in the silence. The air was cool, and the walls were lined with carvings of the moon and stars, each one glowing faintly in the dim light. At the center of the chamber stood a stone altar, its surface smooth and polished, as if it had been waiting for this moment.

Elara approached the altar, her heart pounding in her chest. She could feel the weight of the prophecy pressing down on her, the knowledge that this was the moment that would determine the fate of the world.

Ilyana moved beside her, her hands trembling slightly as she prepared the materials for the ritual. The Moonstone had been shattered, but Selene had given Elara the knowledge she needed to repair it. All that remained was to perform the ritual and restore the balance between the mortal and divine realms.

As they worked, the silver light of the Eternal Moon filled the chamber, casting strange, flickering shadows on the walls. The air was thick with magic, and Elara could feel the power of the moon goddess watching over them.

Finally, the moment came.

Elara placed her hands on the altar, her heart pounding in her chest. She closed her eyes, focusing on the energy around her, on the connection between the mortal and divine realms.

The magic flowed through her, filling her with warmth and light. She could feel the bond between the realms strengthening, the shattered pieces of the Moonstone beginning to knit themselves back together.

But then, something went wrong.

The air grew cold, and the light of the Eternal Moon flickered. Elara's heart raced as she felt the power of the ritual slipping away, as if something was fighting against it, trying to tear the bond apart.

"No," Elara whispered, her voice trembling. "It's not working."

Ilyana's eyes widened in fear. "What's happening?"

Elara shook her head, her mind racing. "I don't know. Something's... something's wrong."

The ground beneath them began to tremble, and the walls of the temple shook. The light of the Eternal Moon flickered wildly, casting strange, twisted shadows across the chamber.

And then, from the darkness, a voice echoed through the temple.

"You cannot stop the Eternal Moon."

Elara's blood ran cold.

The voice was deep, resonant, and filled with an ancient, malevolent power. It echoed through the chamber, sending chills down Elara's spine.

She turned, her heart pounding in her chest.

Standing in the shadows, cloaked in darkness, was a figure. Tall, imposing, and wreathed in the same silvery light that bathed the world.

It was one of the old gods.

And it had come to stop them.

The Eternal Moon was rising, and the fate of the world hung in the balance.

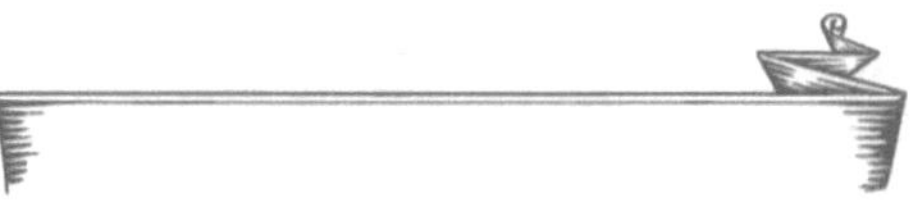

Chapter 10: The Temple of the Moon

The Temple of the Moon stood before them, an imposing relic of an age long forgotten. Its towering spires reached toward the heavens, bathed in the silvery glow of the Eternal Moon that now dominated the sky. The temple was nestled deep within a secluded valley, surrounded by jagged cliffs that seemed to rise like sentinels guarding the ancient structure. Vines clung to its weathered stone walls, and the faint hum of ancient magic pulsed through the air like a heartbeat. It was a place that felt both sacred and dangerous—a place where mortals dared to tread only when the fate of the world hung in the balance.

Elara stood at the entrance, her heart pounding in her chest. She had always known this moment would come, but now that she was here, the weight of her task pressed down on her like a heavy cloak. She and Ilyana had come so far, enduring unimaginable trials and losses along the way. Dorian's betrayal still lingered in her mind, the memory of his final sacrifice cutting deep into her soul. But there was no time to dwell on the past. The Eternal Moon had risen, and the prophecy was unfolding before their eyes. There was no turning back now.

"We've made it," Ilyana said softly, her voice carrying a mix of awe and trepidation. "The Temple of the Moon."

Elara nodded, though her throat felt dry. The wind that swept through the valley was cold, and it carried with it the whispers of the past—echoes of those who had come before them, seeking answers, seeking salvation. But the temple had long since fallen into disuse, forgotten by mortals as the gods faded from their memories. Now, it waited once more for a chosen few to walk its sacred halls.

"We don't have much time," Elara said, her voice steady despite the fear gnawing at her insides. "The Moonstone must be restored before the Eternal Moon reaches its zenith."

Ilyana's gaze flickered to the sky, where the moon hung, larger and more radiant than any moon Elara had ever seen. It was a beautiful sight, but there was something unnatural about it—something that filled Elara with both awe and dread. The magic of the Eternal Moon was ancient and powerful, but it was also dangerous. If the ritual failed, the consequences would be catastrophic.

Without another word, they entered the temple.

The air inside was cool and still, heavy with the scent of old stone and lingering magic. The walls were adorned with faded murals depicting the moon goddess, Selene, and her followers. In some, Selene was shown cradling the moon in her hands, her face serene and wise. In others, she was depicted in battle, wielding the moon's power as a weapon against those who sought to destroy the balance between the mortal and divine realms.

Elara's footsteps echoed as she and Ilyana walked down the long, narrow corridor that led deeper into the temple. The light from the Eternal Moon filtered through cracks in the ceiling, casting ethereal patterns of light and shadow on the stone floor. It felt as though they were walking into another world, a place where time had no meaning and the past and present were woven together.

"We need to be prepared," Ilyana said quietly as they approached the inner sanctum. "The temple is ancient, and its magic is powerful. There will be trials."

Elara glanced at her, the weight of the moment settling in. "What kind of trials?"

"Trials that test more than just our strength," Ilyana replied. "The Temple of the Moon was designed to test the heart, the mind, and the soul. Wisdom, courage, trust—all of these will be required to complete the ritual."

Elara nodded, though a knot of anxiety tightened in her chest. She had faced many challenges on this journey, but this would be different. The temple was not just a physical space—it was a place where the boundaries between the mortal and divine realms blurred. The trials they would face here would push them to their limits, and failure could mean more than just the end of their quest.

As they reached the inner sanctum, the corridor opened into a vast chamber. At the center of the chamber stood a grand altar, the Moon Altar, carved from a single slab of gleaming white stone. The altar was surrounded by towering pillars etched with intricate runes, and at the far end of the room, a set of massive doors loomed, their surfaces covered in ancient symbols. The air was thick with magic, and Elara could feel the power of the temple pressing down on her.

"This is it," Ilyana whispered, her eyes wide with awe. "The Moon Altar."

Elara's gaze settled on the altar, her heart pounding. This was where the Moonstone had to be placed, where the ritual would take place. But something was wrong. The Moonstone was shattered, and without its full power, the ritual could not be completed.

"We have to restore it," Elara said, her voice trembling with determination. "But how?"

Before Ilyana could answer, the chamber began to shift. The floor beneath their feet trembled, and the walls seemed to ripple as if they were made of liquid. Elara stumbled, her hand gripping the hilt of her sword as the air around them shimmered with magic.

Then, from the shadows, a voice echoed through the chamber.

"You who seek the power of the Moonstone, step forward and face the trials."

Elara's breath caught in her throat as the voice reverberated through the chamber. It was a voice unlike any she had ever heard—soft yet commanding, ancient yet familiar. It was the voice of the temple itself, the voice of the gods.

Ilyana stepped forward, her expression calm but tense. "We are ready."

The massive doors at the far end of the chamber began to creak open, revealing a dark passageway beyond. Elara's heart raced as she stared into the darkness, knowing that whatever awaited them beyond those doors would test them in ways they couldn't yet imagine.

Without hesitation, they entered the passageway.

The air inside was cool and damp, the stone walls slick with moisture. The passageway twisted and turned, leading them deeper into the temple's heart. Elara could feel the magic thickening around them, pressing against her skin like a heavy weight. It was as though the temple itself was alive, watching them, waiting to see if they were worthy.

At last, they reached a small chamber. The walls were lined with carvings of the moon in its various phases, and at the center of the room stood a single pedestal, upon which rested a silver chalice. The chalice shimmered in the dim light, its surface etched with the same intricate runes that adorned the pillars in the main chamber.

Ilyana stepped forward, her eyes narrowing as she examined the chalice. "This is the first trial."

Elara frowned. "What are we supposed to do?"

Ilyana gestured to the carvings on the walls. "The phases of the moon. They represent the passage of time, the cycle of life and death, renewal and decay. The chalice is a symbol of that cycle."

Elara studied the carvings, her mind racing. The moon was depicted in its waxing and waning phases, each image representing a different stage in the cycle. But what did it mean? What were they supposed to do?

Before she could speak, the voice of the temple echoed through the chamber once more.

"To restore the Moonstone, you must understand the cycle of the moon. Drink from the chalice, and be prepared to face the truth of what is to come."

Elara's heart pounded as she looked at the chalice. She had no idea what would happen if she drank from it, but there was no other option. They had come too far to turn back now.

"I'll do it," Elara said, her voice steady despite the fear gnawing at her insides.

Ilyana nodded, her expression filled with both concern and trust. "Be careful."

Elara stepped forward and lifted the chalice. The silver felt cold against her skin, and as she raised it to her lips, she hesitated for just a moment. Then, with a deep breath, she drank.

The liquid was cool and smooth, but as soon as it touched her lips, the world around her began to spin. The chamber faded away, and Elara was plunged into darkness.

For a moment, she was weightless, floating in a void of nothingness. Then, slowly, images began to form around her—visions of her past, her present, and her future.

She saw herself as a child, running through the fields near her village, her laughter echoing in the warm summer air. She saw her parents, their faces filled with love and pride as they watched her grow. But then the images shifted, darkened. She saw the day her parents died, the day she had been forced to leave her home behind and venture into the world alone.

Her heart ached as she relived the pain of that loss, but the visions continued. She saw herself on this very journey—meeting Ilyana, fighting alongside Dorian, facing the trials of the gods. And then, she saw the moment of Dorian's betrayal, the moment he had shattered the Moonstone and nearly doomed them all.

But it was the final vision that chilled her to the core.

She saw herself standing at the Moon Altar, the shattered Moonstone in her hands. She saw the light of the Eternal Moon shining down on her, its power overwhelming and terrifying. And she saw herself failing—the ritual slipping out of her grasp as the Eternal Moon's magic consumed the world, plunging it into eternal darkness.

"No," Elara whispered, her voice trembling with fear. "That can't be my future."

The voice of the temple echoed in her mind, soft but unyielding.

"The future is not set in stone. The choices you make will determine your fate."

Elara's heart raced as the vision faded, and she found herself back in the chamber, the chalice still in her hand. She gasped, her chest heaving as she tried to steady herself. The weight of the vision hung heavy on her, the fear of what was to come gnawing at her insides.

"What did you see?" Ilyana asked, her voice filled with concern.

Elara shook her head, her hands trembling as she set the chalice back on the pedestal. "I saw... I saw myself failing. I saw the world consumed by the Eternal Moon."

Ilyana's expression softened, and she placed a reassuring hand on Elara's shoulder. "It was just a vision. The future is not set in stone."

Elara nodded, though the fear still lingered. "I know. But it felt so real."

Ilyana smiled gently. "That's what the trial was meant to do. It was a test of your resolve, your ability to face the truth of what may come. But remember, Elara—you have the power to shape your own fate."

Elara took a deep breath, her heart still racing. The vision had shaken her, but she couldn't let it stop her. The ritual had to be completed, and she had to believe that she could succeed.

"We need to keep going," Elara said, her voice steady once more.

Ilyana nodded, and together they continued down the passageway.

The next trial awaited them in a large, circular chamber. The walls were lined with mirrors, each one reflecting a different version of themselves—some younger, some older, some distorted and twisted. At the center of the chamber stood a pedestal, upon which rested a single, glowing orb.

"The Trial of Reflection," Ilyana said quietly. "This will test our understanding of ourselves—our strengths, our weaknesses, and the choices we've made."

Elara frowned, studying the mirrors. "What do we have to do?"

"The mirrors reflect different versions of ourselves," Ilyana explained. "But not all of them are true. We must choose the reflection that represents our true selves."

Elara's heart pounded as she gazed into the mirrors. She saw herself as a child, carefree and innocent. She saw herself as she was now, battle-worn and weary but determined. And then she saw herself as she might be in the future—older, wiser, but filled with doubt and regret.

"This is a test of trust," Ilyana said. "We must trust in ourselves and in each other to choose the right reflection."

Elara nodded, though the task seemed daunting. How could she know which version of herself was the true one? She had changed so much over the course of this journey, and the person she had been before seemed like a distant memory.

But as she stared into the mirrors, something inside her stirred—a quiet voice that whispered of courage, of hope, and of the strength that came from embracing both her past and her future.

"I trust myself," Elara said, her voice filled with quiet determination. "I know who I am."

With that, she reached out and touched the mirror that reflected her as she was now—battle-worn, weary, but unyielding.

The mirror shimmered, and the orb on the pedestal began to glow brighter.

"You've passed the trial," Ilyana said, her voice filled with quiet pride. "Now, let's complete the ritual."

Elara nodded, her heart pounding with both fear and hope. They had come so far, endured so much, and now the end was in sight.

Together, they returned to the Moon Altar, where the final test awaited.

As Elara placed the Moonstone on the altar, the light of the Eternal Moon flooded the chamber, filling it with a brilliant, silvery glow. The walls seemed to pulse with magic, and the air crackled with energy.

Elara closed her eyes, her hands resting on the Moonstone as she began to chant the words of the ritual—the ancient words that would restore the balance between the mortal and divine realms.

The magic flowed through her, filling her with warmth and light. She could feel the shattered pieces of the Moonstone knitting themselves back together, the power of the moon goddess flowing through her.

But as the ritual reached its climax, Elara felt a tremor in the air—a ripple of dark magic that threatened to tear the ritual apart.

"No!" Elara cried, her voice filled with determination. "I won't let it end this way!"

Summoning all her strength, Elara pushed back against the dark magic, her hands glowing with the light of the moon. The air around her crackled with energy, and the walls of the temple shook as the two forces clashed.

But Elara would not be defeated.

With one final surge of power, the dark magic shattered, and the Moonstone glowed brighter than ever before.

The ritual was complete.

Elara collapsed to her knees, her chest heaving with exhaustion. The air around her was still, the temple bathed in the soft, silver light of the Eternal Moon.

"We did it," Ilyana whispered, her voice filled with awe.

Elara nodded, her heart filled with both relief and exhaustion. They had succeeded. The balance between the mortal and divine realms had been restored.

But the journey was not yet over.

The Eternal Moon still hung in the sky, and the prophecy was not yet fulfilled.

And Elara knew that the hardest trial was yet to come.

Chapter 11: The Arrival of the Old Gods

The Moon Altar was bathed in the pale light of the Eternal Moon, its surface still pulsing with the power of the completed ritual. Elara knelt beside it, her hands trembling from the magic that had coursed through her. The Moonstone lay in the center, its once-shattered pieces now whole again, glowing softly as it restored balance between the mortal and divine realms.

But even as the power of the moon goddess, Selene, flowed through her, Elara felt a growing unease. The air around them had shifted. The comforting light of the Moonstone felt fragile, as though it was fighting against something far darker, something far more ancient than even Selene herself.

Ilyana stood at her side, her face pale and drawn, her eyes darting around the temple as if searching for something just beyond the shadows. "Something's wrong," she whispered, her voice barely audible. "I can feel it."

Elara nodded, her heart pounding. She could feel it too. The magic in the air had thickened, growing heavier and more oppressive. It was as if the temple itself was holding its breath, waiting for something to happen—something terrible.

And then, it did.

The ground beneath them trembled, a deep, ominous rumble that reverberated through the stone walls of the temple. Elara stumbled to her feet, her eyes wide as the Moonstone's light flickered, dimming for the first time since the ritual had begun. The temperature dropped suddenly, the air becoming frigid and thin, as though the very life was being sucked out of the space around them.

From the far end of the chamber, where the shadows were thickest, a figure began to emerge.

Elara's breath caught in her throat as the figure stepped into the light. It was taller than any human, its body wrapped in tattered robes that shimmered like the night sky. Its face was hidden beneath a hood, but its eyes glowed with an intense, otherworldly light—two burning orbs that seemed to pierce through Elara's very soul.

"The old gods," Ilyana whispered, her voice filled with fear and awe. "They've come."

The figure moved slowly, deliberately, its steps echoing through the chamber like the tolling of a great bell. And behind it, more figures emerged from the shadows—gods and goddesses of ancient legend, long forgotten by mortals but still brimming with power.

Elara could feel their presence like a physical force, pressing down on her chest, making it hard to breathe. These were not the gods of mercy and wisdom that she had been taught to revere in her childhood. These were the old gods—beings of raw, untamed power, whose dominion over the world had been absolute before they were cast into the shadows by their own kind.

They moved closer, their eyes fixed on the Moonstone, their intentions clear.

Elara stepped in front of the altar, her heart racing as she faced them. "I won't let you take it," she said, her voice stronger than she felt. "The balance has been restored. The prophecy will be fulfilled, but not in your favor."

The lead god—the one who had first emerged from the shadows—let out a low, rumbling laugh that sent chills down Elara's spine. "You speak of balance, mortal," he said, his voice deep and resonant, like the grinding of stone. "But you do not understand what true balance is. You are merely a pawn, playing a game far beyond your comprehension."

Elara clenched her fists, standing her ground. "I understand enough. You want to use the Eternal Moon to reclaim your power, to dominate the mortal world again. But I won't let you."

The god's eyes narrowed, glowing brighter. "You think you can stand against us? Against the gods who shaped this world from nothingness? You are nothing, mortal."

Ilyana stepped forward, her voice steady despite the fear that Elara could see in her eyes. "Elara may be mortal, but she has the power of the moon goddess, Selene, flowing through her. She has restored the Moonstone and the balance between the realms. You have no right to take it from her."

The god's gaze shifted to Ilyana, and for a moment, the chamber was filled with a heavy silence. Then, with a flick of his hand, the god sent a wave of dark energy toward her. Ilyana was thrown back against the wall, the impact knocking the wind from her lungs.

"Ilyana!" Elara cried, rushing to her side.

Ilyana groaned, clutching her ribs as she struggled to sit up. "I'm... I'm fine," she gasped, though her face was pale with pain. "We need to stop them."

Elara turned back to the gods, her heart pounding. The lead god had stepped closer to the altar, his eyes fixed on the Moonstone as if drawn to its power. Elara could feel the energy in the air growing more unstable, the balance she had fought so hard to restore slipping away with each passing moment.

"You cannot stop us," the god said, his voice filled with cold certainty. "The prophecy is ours to fulfill. We will reclaim what is rightfully ours, and the world of mortals will bow before us once more."

Elara's heart raced as the god raised his hand, a swirling vortex of dark magic forming around him. The other gods stood behind him, their eyes glowing with anticipation, as though they were watching a long-awaited event unfold.

But Elara refused to give up. She had come too far, fought too hard, to let the old gods win now. She could feel the power of Selene within her, the moon goddess's magic still strong despite the overwhelming presence of the old gods. She wasn't alone in this fight.

"You're wrong," Elara said, her voice steady. "This isn't your world anymore. The time of the old gods is over."

With a surge of determination, Elara raised her hands, calling on the power of the Moonstone. The altar began to glow brighter, the silver light pulsing as the energy of the Eternal Moon filled the chamber. The air crackled with magic, and for a moment, the old gods hesitated, their eyes narrowing as they felt the strength of the power Elara wielded.

But the lead god let out a deep, mocking laugh. "Foolish mortal. You think the power of a single goddess can stand against us?"

Elara's heart pounded in her chest, but she refused to back down. "I don't need to stand against you. I need to protect this world from you."

The god's eyes flashed with anger, and he raised his hand again, sending another wave of dark energy toward Elara. But this time, Elara was ready. She raised her own hand, and the light of the Moonstone flared, meeting the dark energy head-on. The two forces collided with a deafening crack, sending shockwaves through the temple.

The other gods stepped forward, their eyes glowing with fury. They began to chant in a language Elara didn't understand, their voices blending together in a low, ominous hum. The air around them shimmered with dark magic, and Elara could feel the weight of their power pressing down on her, threatening to crush her.

But she couldn't give up. She had to protect the Moonstone, protect the balance. She had to stop the old gods from reclaiming their dominance over the mortal world.

"Ilyana!" Elara called, her voice strained. "I need your help!"

Ilyana struggled to her feet, her face pale but determined. She limped toward Elara, her hand glowing with healing magic as she touched Elara's shoulder. "I'm with you."

Together, they faced the old gods, their combined magic swirling around them like a protective barrier. The gods' chanting grew louder, their voices rising to a fever pitch as they summoned more and more power. The ground beneath them trembled, and cracks began to form in the walls of the temple.

Elara could feel the strain of the magic coursing through her, the weight of the power she was wielding almost too much to bear. But she couldn't let the gods win. She couldn't let them take control of the world again.

"We can't hold them off forever," Ilyana gasped, her voice filled with urgency. "We need to finish the ritual."

Elara nodded, her heart pounding. "How?"

Ilyana's eyes flickered to the Moonstone, still glowing on the altar. "We need to bind the power of the Moonstone to the mortal realm, severing the old gods' connection to it."

Elara swallowed hard. It was a dangerous plan—one that could backfire if they didn't do it correctly. But it was their only chance.

"Let's do it," Elara said, her voice filled with determination.

Ilyana began to chant, her hands glowing with magic as she prepared the final part of the ritual. Elara focused on the Moonstone, drawing on its power as she channeled the energy through her body.

The old gods, sensing what they were trying to do, roared in anger. The lead god stepped forward, his eyes blazing with fury. "You cannot defy us!"

Elara gritted her teeth, her body trembling with the effort of holding back the gods' magic. "Watch us."

With a final surge of power, Elara and Ilyana completed the ritual. The Moonstone flared with blinding light, its energy pulsing through the temple and out into the world. The old gods screamed in rage as the light enveloped them, their forms flickering and fading as the bond between them and the mortal realm was severed.

The ground beneath them shook violently, and for a moment, Elara thought the temple would collapse. But then, just as suddenly as it had begun, the shaking stopped. The light of the Moonstone dimmed, and the old gods were gone.

Elara collapsed to her knees, her body trembling with exhaustion. The air around them was still, the oppressive weight of the gods' presence lifted. The Eternal Moon still hung in the sky, but its light was softer now, less menacing.

Ilyana knelt beside her, her hand on Elara's shoulder. "We did it."

Elara nodded, though her heart was heavy with the knowledge of what had just happened. They had won, but the battle had taken its toll. The old gods had been defeated, but at what cost?

"I don't know what the future holds," Elara said quietly, her voice filled with both relief and uncertainty. "But at least we stopped them. At least we gave the world a chance."

Ilyana smiled faintly, though her eyes were filled with weariness. "You did more than that, Elara. You changed the world."

Elara looked up at the Moonstone, its soft glow a reminder of the power she had wielded, the power she had fought to protect. The gods' presence was gone, but their influence would linger for a long time to come.

As the light of the Eternal Moon bathed the temple in a soft, silvery glow, Elara couldn't help but wonder what kind of world they had saved—and what kind of world they had created.

But for now, the battle was over.

And the fate of the world was in their hands.

Chapter 12: The Shadow of the Night God

The air inside the Temple of the Moon was still thick with magic, but now there was an unsettling calm that permeated the space. The old gods had been banished, their connection to the mortal realm severed, and the Moonstone had been restored. Yet, as Elara stood before the Moon Altar, her heart heavy with the weight of everything she had faced, she couldn't shake the feeling that something was still wrong—something lurking just beyond the edge of her awareness, waiting for the perfect moment to strike.

The silver light of the Eternal Moon bathed the temple in a soft, ethereal glow, but it did little to comfort Elara. Her mind raced as she considered everything that had happened, and the strange sense of unfinished business gnawed at her insides.

Ilyana, standing beside her, seemed to sense it too. "We've stopped the old gods," she said, her voice quiet but steady. "But the moon... it hasn't changed."

Elara followed Ilyana's gaze to the sky. The Eternal Moon still hung high above them, larger than ever, its radiant glow unyielding. The moon's light had not dimmed or shifted, and the oppressive magic that had filled the air since the prophecy began had not abated. It was as if something was holding the moon in place, preventing the balance from being fully restored.

"Why hasn't it ended?" Elara asked, her voice barely above a whisper. "We completed the ritual. The old gods are gone. The Moonstone is whole again."

Ilyana shook her head, her brows furrowing in concern. "I don't know. But something... something's still wrong."

Elara's heart pounded in her chest as a chilling realization crept over her. The old gods had been banished, but the Eternal Moon remained. That could only mean one thing: there was another force at play, something far more dangerous than they had anticipated.

Suddenly, the temperature in the temple plummeted. A cold, unnatural wind swept through the chamber, swirling around them like a living thing. The soft glow of the Moonstone flickered, and the shadows that had clung to the corners of the room began to shift and writhe, growing darker and more pronounced.

Ilyana gasped, her eyes widening as the shadows seemed to coalesce into a single, towering figure. The air crackled with dark energy, and Elara could feel the weight of a presence unlike any she had felt before—one that was ancient, powerful, and utterly malevolent.

From the depths of the shadows, a voice echoed through the chamber, deep and resonant, filled with an unsettling calm.

"You think you've won, little mortal?"

Elara's blood ran cold as the figure stepped forward, emerging from the shadows like a creature born of the night itself. He was tall and imposing, his body draped in a cloak of darkness that seemed to absorb the light around him. His face was obscured by a hood, but his eyes—glowing a deep, inky black—burned with an intensity that sent chills down Elara's spine.

"I am Nyxos," the figure said, his voice carrying the weight of ages. "God of the Night. Master of the shadows. And you have only just begun to understand the true nature of the prophecy."

Elara's heart pounded in her chest as she stared at the being before her. This was no ordinary god—this was the Night God himself, the very embodiment of darkness and shadow. And the power radiating from him was overwhelming, suffocating.

Ilyana took a step back, her face pale with fear. "Nyxos... the god of eternal night."

Elara's mind raced as she tried to make sense of it all. Nyxos had been behind the prophecy all along. He had orchestrated everything—the rise of the Eternal Moon, the return of the old gods, the battle for control of the Moonstone. But why? What did he want?

Nyxos chuckled softly, as if reading her thoughts. "You still don't understand, do you, Elara? The Eternal Moon is not merely a celestial event. It is a gateway—a gateway through which I will reclaim my dominion over the world. The night will never end, and I will reign supreme, as it was always meant to be."

Elara's heart raced as the full weight of his words sank in. Nyxos didn't just want to reclaim power like the other old gods—he wanted to plunge the world into eternal darkness, to hold dominion over the night and everything within it. The Eternal Moon was his key to doing that.

But what chilled her even more was the way he spoke her name, as if he knew her intimately.

"I've been watching you, Elara," Nyxos said, his voice a low purr. "You are different from the others. You have power, more power than you realize. And that power comes from me."

Elara's breath caught in her throat. "What are you talking about?"

Nyxos took a step closer, his glowing eyes never leaving hers. "You have always felt it, haven't you? The connection to the night, to the shadows. The way darkness calls to you, the way it empowers you."

Elara shook her head, her heart pounding. "No. That's not true."

Nyxos smiled, though there was no warmth in it. "You can deny it all you want, but the truth remains. You were born of the night, Elara. You carry my essence within you."

Elara's mind reeled. This couldn't be true. She wasn't connected to Nyxos—she wasn't a part of his plan. She had been fighting to stop the prophecy, to restore balance. She couldn't be tied to him.

But deep down, a part of her knew that Nyxos wasn't lying. There had always been something inside her—something dark, something powerful—that she had never fully understood. She had felt it throughout her journey, in the moments of greatest danger, when her instincts had sharpened and her strength had surged. It was as if the shadows themselves had lent her their power.

And now, she knew why.

Nyxos watched her intently, his eyes gleaming with satisfaction. "You are more like me than you are willing to admit. You have the power to shape the night, to bend the shadows to your will. You could stand by my side, Elara. Together, we could rule the night."

Elara's heart pounded in her chest. "I won't join you. I won't help you plunge the world into darkness."

Nyxos's smile faded, and his expression grew serious. "You misunderstand, Elara. This is not a request. This is your destiny. You are meant to rule the night with me. The Eternal Moon will remain in the sky, and the world will be ours."

Elara shook her head, her mind racing. "No. I won't do it."

Nyxos's eyes narrowed, and the air around them grew colder. "You think you have a choice in this? The power you possess is not something you can simply reject. It is a part of you, just as the night is a part of me."

Elara's hands trembled as she felt the darkness within her stir, responding to Nyxos's words. He was right—she could feel it, the pull of the night, the power of the shadows coursing through her veins. But she couldn't give in to it. She couldn't let Nyxos control her.

"I won't let you win," Elara said, her voice trembling but determined. "I may have your power, but I am not yours."

Nyxos's expression darkened, and the shadows around him seemed to grow thicker, more oppressive. "You are a fool, Elara. You cannot fight against your own nature. You cannot fight against me."

Elara's heart raced as Nyxos raised his hand, and the shadows around them surged forward, wrapping around her like tendrils of darkness. The cold, suffocating weight of the night pressed down on her, and she could feel the darkness within her rising, threatening to consume her.

But she couldn't give in. She had come too far, fought too hard, to let Nyxos take control now.

With a surge of willpower, Elara reached deep within herself, drawing on the power of the Moonstone and the light of the Eternal Moon. The darkness inside her recoiled, and the shadows that had wrapped around her began to dissipate, fading back into the night.

Nyxos's eyes flashed with anger, and he took a step closer, his voice a low growl. "You think you can resist me? You are nothing without the night."

Elara's breath came in ragged gasps, but she stood her ground. "I am not nothing. And I am not yours to control."

Nyxos raised his hand again, and this time the darkness surged toward her with even greater force, the shadows twisting and writhing like a living thing. Elara braced herself, her hands glowing with the light of the Moonstone as she fought back against the onslaught.

The two forces collided—Nyxos's dark, oppressive magic against the pure, radiant light of the Moonstone—and the temple shook with the force of the clash. The air crackled with energy, and Elara could feel the strain of holding back Nyxos's power. It was like trying to hold back the tide, an overwhelming force that threatened to crush her.

But she couldn't give up. She couldn't let him win.

With a cry of determination, Elara pushed back against the darkness, her light flaring brighter and stronger. The shadows around her began to recede, and she could feel Nyxos's power wavering, his control slipping.

"You are not as powerful as you think, Nyxos," Elara said, her voice filled with defiance. "You may control the night, but I control my own fate."

Nyxos's eyes burned with fury, and for a moment, it seemed as though he would strike again, his hand clenched into a fist. But then, slowly, the darkness around him began to fade. The shadows retreated, and the oppressive weight of his presence lifted.

For a long moment, the two of them stood in silence, the tension between them crackling like lightning in the air.

"You are a fool, Elara," Nyxos said, his voice low and dangerous. "You could have had everything. Power, immortality, control over the night itself. But you chose weakness. You chose to fight against your own nature."

Elara's heart pounded in her chest, but she met his gaze without fear. "I chose to fight for what is right. I chose to fight for the light."

Nyxos sneered, his eyes filled with disdain. "The light will not save you. The Eternal Moon will rise, and the world will be plunged into eternal night. You cannot stop it."

Elara's hands trembled, but she refused to back down. "We'll see about that."

Without another word, Nyxos turned and disappeared into the shadows, his form dissolving into the darkness as if he had never been there at all.

The air around them stilled, the oppressive magic fading with Nyxos's departure. Elara stood in the silence of the temple, her heart pounding and her body trembling from the strain of the battle.

Ilyana rushed to her side, her face pale with concern. "Elara, are you all right?"

Elara nodded, though her body ached with exhaustion. "I'm fine. But Nyxos... he's not gone. He'll be back."

Ilyana's eyes widened. "What do we do?"

Elara looked up at the Moonstone, its soft glow a reminder of the power she had fought to protect. Nyxos may have been the mastermind behind the prophecy, but she wasn't going to let him win. She wasn't going to let the world be plunged into eternal night.

"We stop him," Elara said, her voice filled with quiet determination. "We finish what we started."

The shadows of the night still lingered, but Elara knew that the light of the moon would guide her.

And no matter how strong the darkness was, she wouldn't let it consume her.

The battle against Nyxos was far from over, but Elara was ready.

Chapter 13: The Ritual of the Eternal Moon

The wind howled through the hollowed halls of the Temple of the Moon, carrying with it the weight of ancient magic and impending doom. The silvery glow of the Eternal Moon illuminated the space with an ethereal light that danced over the stone walls, casting long shadows that seemed to shift and move of their own accord. It was as though the temple itself were alive, breathing in the power of the moon and the magic that had been woven into its very stones for centuries.

Elara stood before the Moon Altar, her hands resting on its cool, smooth surface. The Moonstone, glowing faintly in the dim light, sat at the center of the altar, its fractured surface a reminder of the peril they now faced. The gods had been banished, but Nyxos, the Night God, remained—his power growing stronger with every passing moment as the Eternal Moon hung above them, refusing to wane.

She could feel the weight of the ritual pressing down on her, the ancient magic swirling around her like a heavy cloak. The words of Selene, the moon goddess, echoed in her mind: *The Eternal Moon must be restored. The balance between the mortal and divine realms must be repaired.*

But the cost... the cost was too great to bear.

Elara's heart pounded in her chest as the realization of what had to be done sank in. The ritual required a sacrifice. Not just any sacrifice, but the life of the one who carried the Moonstone. The one who had been chosen to restore balance. The one who had fought so hard to stop the prophecy from coming true.

Her.

Elara took a deep, steadying breath, her hands trembling as she stared at the glowing Moonstone. She had known from the beginning that this journey would be dangerous, that the prophecy carried with it the risk of losing everything. But she hadn't realized that it would come to this—that she would be the one to give her life to save the world.

The thought of it filled her with a deep, aching sorrow. She had fought so hard, come so far, and now, at the very end, she had to make the ultimate sacrifice.

"I can't do this," Elara whispered, her voice trembling with fear and uncertainty. "I can't."

Beside her, Ilyana stood silent, her eyes filled with understanding and pain. The healer had always been strong, a pillar of wisdom and comfort throughout their journey. But now, Elara could see the same fear mirrored in her friend's eyes—the fear of what was to come, the fear of losing someone she loved.

"Elara," Ilyana said softly, her voice steady but filled with emotion. "You don't have to do this alone."

Elara shook her head, tears welling in her eyes. "But I do. The prophecy... the Moonstone... it all leads to this. I have to be the one to complete the ritual. It's my fate."

Ilyana's eyes softened, and she stepped closer, placing a comforting hand on Elara's shoulder. "Fate is not always set in stone. You have the power to choose your own path."

Elara's heart ached as she looked at her friend, the weight of her choice pressing down on her like a physical burden. She had never wanted this. She had never wanted to be the one to carry the weight of the world on her shoulders. But now, standing at the edge of the abyss, she knew there was no other way.

"I don't want to die," Elara whispered, her voice breaking. "I don't want to leave you."

Ilyana's expression softened, and she squeezed Elara's shoulder gently. "I know. But sometimes, the hardest choices are the ones that matter the most."

Elara closed her eyes, her heart pounding in her chest. The air around them was thick with magic, and she could feel the pull of the ritual calling to her, demanding that she fulfill her role. The Moonstone pulsed with a faint light, as if it, too, understood the gravity of the moment.

The ritual had to be completed. The balance had to be restored. The Eternal Moon had to be brought down from the sky.

But at what cost?

Elara opened her eyes, her gaze settling on the Moonstone. It glowed softly, its fractured surface shimmering in the light of the Eternal Moon. This was the key to everything. This was the only way to stop Nyxos and the other gods from reclaiming their power.

And it required her life.

With a deep, steadying breath, Elara stepped forward, her hands hovering over the Moonstone. She could feel its magic coursing through her, a steady pulse of energy that resonated with her very soul. This was it. This was the moment she had been dreading.

"I'm ready," Elara said softly, her voice barely above a whisper. "I'm ready to do what needs to be done."

But before she could lower her hands to the Moonstone, Ilyana stepped in front of her, her eyes filled with fierce determination. "No, Elara. You don't have to do this."

Elara frowned, confusion and fear swirling in her chest. "What are you talking about? Ilyana, I'm the one who has to do this. It's my destiny."

Ilyana shook her head, her expression resolute. "No. It's not your destiny. It doesn't have to be."

Elara's heart raced as she stared at her friend, her mind struggling to process what she was hearing. "Ilyana, please... I don't understand."

Ilyana's eyes softened, and she took Elara's hands in her own, her voice gentle but firm. "I've watched you fight, Elara. I've watched you carry the weight of this prophecy on your shoulders, and I've seen how much it has cost you. You've given everything to save this world, to stop the gods from taking control. But you don't have to give your life."

Elara shook her head, tears streaming down her cheeks. "But the ritual... it requires a sacrifice. It has to be me."

"No," Ilyana said, her voice filled with quiet conviction. "It doesn't. It can be anyone who is willing to give their life for the balance. And I am willing."

Elara's breath caught in her throat, her heart lurching in her chest. "No, Ilyana. You can't. I won't let you."

But Ilyana smiled softly, her eyes filled with love and sadness. "You've already given so much, Elara. You've already sacrificed so much. Let me do this. Let me be the one to complete the ritual."

Elara's mind reeled, her heart breaking at the thought of losing her friend. "Ilyana, please... I can't lose you."

Ilyana's smile wavered, and for a moment, Elara saw the same fear in her friend's eyes that she had felt in her own heart. But Ilyana's resolve was unshakable.

"You won't lose me," Ilyana said softly. "I'll always be with you. And you'll go on to live the life you deserve. A life where you're not burdened by the weight of this prophecy."

Elara shook her head, her tears falling freely now. "I don't want that life without you."

Ilyana's expression softened, and she pulled Elara into a tight embrace, holding her close. "You will live, Elara. You will find happiness. And you will remember me, not as a sacrifice, but as your friend who loved you."

Elara sobbed against Ilyana's shoulder, her heart shattering at the thought of what was about to happen. She didn't want this. She didn't want to lose Ilyana, the one person who had been with her through it all. But deep down, she knew there was no stopping her friend.

"I love you," Elara whispered, her voice trembling with grief. "I love you so much."

Ilyana smiled through her own tears. "And I love you. That's why I have to do this."

With a final, lingering embrace, Ilyana pulled away, her eyes filled with a quiet determination. She stepped forward, her hands hovering over the Moonstone, the soft glow of its magic reflecting in her tear-streaked face.

Elara watched, her heart breaking, as Ilyana prepared herself for the ritual. The air around them crackled with energy, and the light of the Eternal Moon grew brighter, casting long, eerie shadows across the temple walls.

"Ilyana, please," Elara whispered, her voice barely audible. "Don't do this."

But Ilyana only smiled softly, her hands lowering to rest on the Moonstone. "It's all right, Elara. I'm ready."

As soon as her hands touched the surface of the stone, the magic of the temple surged to life, filling the chamber with a blinding light. The walls trembled, and the air hummed with the power of the ritual as it began to unfold.

Elara felt the pull of the magic, the ancient forces that had been set in motion long before she was born. She could feel the power of the Moonstone coursing through Ilyana, binding her to the ritual, drawing her into the heart of the magic that would restore balance to the world.

But with that power came the cost—the ultimate price that had to be paid.

Elara watched in horror as Ilyana's body began to glow, her form shimmering with the light of the Eternal Moon. The air around her friend crackled with energy, and Elara could see the toll the ritual was taking on her, the life slowly draining from her body as the magic consumed her.

"Ilyana!" Elara cried, her voice filled with anguish.

But Ilyana didn't falter. Her eyes met Elara's, and in that moment, Elara saw the love and peace that radiated from her friend. There was no fear, no regret—only acceptance.

With a final, shuddering breath, Ilyana whispered, "It's done."

The light of the Moonstone flared, blinding in its intensity, and for a moment, Elara was consumed by the brilliance of the magic that filled the temple. The ground beneath her feet shook, and the walls of the temple groaned as the power of the ritual reached its peak.

And then, just as suddenly as it had begun, it was over.

The light faded, and the air around them stilled. The temple was silent, the oppressive magic of the Eternal Moon lifted. The Moonstone, once fractured, now glowed with a soft, steady light—a beacon of balance and peace.

But Ilyana was gone.

Elara collapsed to her knees, her heart breaking as the weight of her loss crashed over her. The temple was still, the air cold and empty without Ilyana's presence. She had given her life to save the world, to restore the balance between the mortal and divine realms. And now, she was gone.

Sobs wracked Elara's body as she knelt before the Moonstone, her tears falling onto the cold stone floor. The world had been saved, but the cost had been too great.

"Ilyana," Elara whispered, her voice broken. "Why did it have to be you?"

But there was no answer. Only the soft glow of the Moonstone, and the memory of a friend who had loved her enough to give everything.

The Eternal Moon had set, the balance had been restored, and the gods had been sealed away once more.

But Elara's heart would never be the same.

Chapter 14: The Dawn After the Eternal Night

The first rays of sunlight crept over the horizon, casting a warm, golden glow over the world. For the first time in what felt like an eternity, the darkness was lifting. The Eternal Moon, once an oppressive presence in the sky, had faded, its silvery light replaced by the natural cycle of day and night. The magic that had held the world in its grip for so long was finally receding, and the world was beginning to heal.

Elara stood at the edge of a cliff overlooking the valley below, her heart heavy with both grief and relief. The ritual had been completed. The balance between the mortal and divine realms had been restored, and the Eternal Moon had been brought down from the sky. But the cost... the cost had been more than she had ever imagined.

Ilyana was gone.

The thought of her friend's sacrifice weighed on Elara's soul like a stone. She had known from the moment Ilyana had stepped forward that there was no stopping her, that her friend had made her choice. But it didn't make the loss any easier to bear. Ilyana had given everything to save the world, and now she was gone, leaving behind an emptiness that Elara wasn't sure she would ever be able to fill.

The wind stirred gently, rustling the leaves of the trees that lined the cliffside. The air was cool and crisp, carrying with it the scent of the earth after a long, heavy rain. It was a peaceful morning, the kind of morning that seemed to promise new beginnings, a fresh start. But for Elara, it felt like the end of something important.

She had stood on this very cliff before, not long ago, when the Eternal Moon had first begun its rise. Back then, the world had been on the brink of chaos, with the old gods stirring from their slumber and the prophecy hanging over her like a dark cloud. She had been uncertain, afraid, unsure of what her role in all of it was supposed to be.

Now, as she stood here again, the world felt different. The threat of the old gods had passed, the Eternal Moon had faded, and the balance had been restored. But the journey had left its mark on her—both physically and emotionally. She was not the same person who had stood on this cliff before. She had faced darkness, both within herself and in the world, and come out the other side. But the cost had been high.

Elara closed her eyes, taking a deep breath as she tried to steady herself. The weight of Ilyana's sacrifice pressed down on her, making it hard to breathe. She had always known that this journey would require sacrifices, but she hadn't expected to lose the one person who had been with her through it all. Ilyana had been more than a friend—she had been her anchor, her guide, the person who had kept her grounded when everything else felt like it was falling apart.

"Ilyana," Elara whispered, her voice breaking. "Why did you have to go?"

The wind carried her words away, leaving only the soft rustling of the trees and the distant sound of birdsong. The world was moving on, healing from the chaos that had been unleashed by the return of the gods. But Elara's heart still felt heavy, weighed down by the loss of her friend.

Behind her, the sound of footsteps approached, and Elara turned to see a familiar figure walking toward her. It was Dorian, the warrior who had fought by her side for so long. His face was solemn, his expression a mirror of the grief that Elara felt in her own heart.

"Elara," Dorian said softly, his voice filled with empathy. "I thought I might find you here."

Elara nodded, turning back to face the horizon. "It's strange, isn't it? How the world can feel so peaceful after everything that's happened."

Dorian stepped up beside her, his gaze following hers to the sunrise. "It feels like the end of one story and the beginning of another."

Elara let out a soft sigh, her heart aching. "Ilyana should be here. She should be standing with us, seeing this new beginning."

Dorian placed a comforting hand on her shoulder. "I know. She was a great healer, and an even greater friend. Her sacrifice... it saved us all."

Elara swallowed hard, her throat tight with emotion. "I just can't stop thinking that it should have been me. I was the one meant to complete the ritual. I was the one who carried the Moonstone."

Dorian shook his head gently. "Ilyana made her choice, Elara. She knew what she was doing. She gave her life so that you could live, so that the world could be saved. Don't dishonor her sacrifice by doubting it."

Elara nodded, though the ache in her heart remained. "I just... I don't know how to move forward without her."

Dorian's expression softened, and he turned to face her fully. "You don't have to forget her. You don't have to move on without her. You can carry her with you, in your heart, in your memories. She'll always be a part of you, Elara. And her sacrifice... it will be remembered for generations to come."

Elara closed her eyes, letting the words sink in. Dorian was right. Ilyana's sacrifice had not been in vain. The world was healing, the natural order was being restored, and the connection between mortals and the divine had been renewed—but in a way that fostered cooperation and understanding, rather than domination. Ilyana had given her life to make that possible.

"I'll never forget her," Elara said softly, her voice filled with quiet determination. "I'll make sure that no one ever forgets her."

Dorian smiled gently, his hand still resting on her shoulder. "She'd want that."

For a long moment, they stood in silence, watching as the sun continued its ascent into the sky. The light of the new day washed over the valley, illuminating the landscape with a soft, golden glow. The world was quiet, peaceful, as if it were taking a collective breath after the chaos of the past days.

As the sun rose higher, Elara could see the signs of healing all around them. The forests that had been twisted and warped by the magic of the Eternal Moon were beginning to return to their natural state, the trees no longer casting strange, unnatural shadows. The creatures that had been stirred from their slumber by the rise of the old gods were retreating to their realms, their presence no longer threatening the balance of the world.

The connection between mortals and the divine remained, but it had changed. The gods no longer sought to dominate or control the mortal world. Instead, there was a sense of cooperation, a mutual understanding that the two realms were meant to coexist in harmony. The balance that had been restored was fragile, but it was a start—a new beginning.

"I think the world is going to be different now," Elara said quietly, her gaze still fixed on the horizon. "Not just because of the gods, but because of us."

Dorian nodded in agreement. "We've shown that mortals can stand up to the gods, that we can shape our own destiny. I think that's something the gods will remember."

Elara smiled faintly, though her heart still ached with the weight of loss. "Maybe it's a new era. One where we're not just pawns in their games."

Dorian's smile widened slightly, a spark of hope in his eyes. "Maybe."

They stood in silence for a while longer, the peaceful morning stretching out before them. Elara's thoughts drifted back to Ilyana, and she felt a pang of sorrow in her chest. But there was also a sense of peace—a peace that came from knowing that her friend's sacrifice had made all of this possible. The world was healing, and the balance had been restored. Ilyana's life had not been lost in vain.

"I'm going to keep moving," Elara said softly, her voice filled with quiet determination. "There's so much more to do. So many lives to help rebuild. I can't just stand still."

Dorian looked at her, his expression thoughtful. "What will you do now? Where will you go?"

Elara took a deep breath, the weight of the question settling over her. She had spent so long fighting, so long focused on the prophecy and the threat of the gods, that she hadn't had time to think about what came after. But now, with the Eternal Moon gone and the balance restored, she had a chance to start over.

"I don't know yet," she admitted, her voice soft. "But I think I'll go where I'm needed. There are a lot of people out there who've been affected by all of this—people who need help rebuilding their lives. Ilyana would have wanted me to help them."

Dorian nodded, his expression filled with understanding. "And you'll do great things, Elara. I know you will."

Elara smiled faintly, though her heart still felt heavy with the weight of loss. "I hope so."

As the morning sun continued to rise, Elara turned away from the cliff and began to walk back toward the temple, Dorian following closely behind. The Temple of the Moon, once a place of uncertainty and fear, now felt like a place of peace—a place where the world had been saved and where the future had been shaped.

The old gods had been sealed away once more, and the connection between the mortal and divine realms had been renewed. But this time, the balance was different. Mortals were no longer at the mercy of the gods. They had proven that they could stand on their own, that they could shape their own destiny.

As they reached the entrance of the temple, Elara paused, her gaze lingering on the ancient stone walls. The temple had been the site of so many battles, so many sacrifices. But it had also been the place where the world had been saved.

"Ilyana," Elara whispered, her voice filled with love and sorrow. "I'll carry your memory with me, always."

With one final, lingering glance at the temple, Elara turned and began to walk away, her heart filled with both grief and hope. The world was healing, and though the pain of Ilyana's loss would never fully fade, Elara knew that her friend's sacrifice had made all of this possible.

The dawn after the Eternal Night had come, and with it, a new beginning.

Elara's journey was far from over, but as she walked into the light of the new day, she knew that she would carry Ilyana's memory with her, always.

And in that, there was peace.

Chapter 15: The Legend of the Eternal Moon

The village of Eldwyn had always been quiet, nestled in a valley untouched by the grandeur of the world beyond. Its people were humble, their lives simple, and the legends of ancient gods and forgotten powers had always felt distant, like tales told to children by the fireside on cold nights. But now, as Elara walked along the familiar path that led to the village, everything felt different. She was different.

The sun hung low in the sky, casting a golden glow over the fields that stretched out around her. The gentle breeze rustled the tall grass, carrying with it the scent of the earth after a fresh rain. Birds sang from the trees, and in the distance, she could hear the faint murmur of the river that had always been the lifeblood of the village. It was a scene so familiar, so unchanged from the days before her journey had begun, yet it no longer felt like the same place.

Elara paused at the crest of the hill, gazing down at the village below. The houses, with their thatched roofs and stone walls, seemed smaller now, almost fragile in their simplicity. The people who lived there went about their daily lives, unaware of the great forces that had nearly torn the world apart. They had no idea of the sacrifices that had been made, the battles fought in the shadows, to protect their way of life.

For a moment, Elara felt a pang of sadness. She had always dreamed of returning to Eldwyn, of coming home after her long journey, but now that she was here, it didn't feel like home anymore. She had changed. The world had changed. And there was no going back to the way things had been.

With a deep breath, she continued down the path, her footsteps slow and deliberate. The weight of the Moonstone was no longer with her, but the burden of everything she had experienced still lingered in her heart. The memory of Ilyana's sacrifice, the battles with the old gods, the overwhelming power of the Eternal Moon—all of it was still fresh in her mind, like scars that had yet to fully heal.

As she approached the village, a few of the villagers noticed her, their expressions shifting from curiosity to recognition. Murmurs spread through the small crowd, and soon, people began to gather at the edge of the village, watching as Elara made her way down the path. She could see the questions in their eyes, the unspoken awe in their expressions.

"Elara," a voice called out, and she turned to see Old Liora, the village elder, making her way toward her. The old woman's face was lined with age, but her eyes were sharp and clear, filled with the wisdom of someone who had seen more than most.

Elara smiled softly, though her heart was heavy. "Liora."

The elder stopped before her, studying her with a gaze that seemed to see straight through her. "You've been gone a long time, child."

Elara nodded, her voice quiet. "Longer than I expected."

"And you've come back changed." It wasn't a question, but a statement of fact.

Elara looked away, her gaze drifting to the distant horizon. "Yes. The world... it's different now. And so am I."

Liora's expression softened, and she placed a hand on Elara's arm. "Come. Tell us what you've seen, what you've done. The village needs to hear your story."

Elara hesitated, unsure if she was ready to share everything that had happened. But as she looked into Liora's eyes, she realized that the story of the Eternal Moon wasn't just hers—it belonged to the world. It was a story that needed to be told, not just for the sake of those who had lived through it, but for the generations to come.

With a nod, she followed Liora into the heart of the village. A fire had been lit in the center of the square, and the villagers gathered around, their faces illuminated by the flickering flames. Children sat at the front, their eyes wide with anticipation, while the adults stood behind them, their expressions a mixture of curiosity and concern.

Elara stood before them, feeling the weight of their expectations. She had always been just another villager, a quiet girl who had lived a simple life. But now, as she looked into their faces, she realized that she had become something more—a symbol of hope, a reminder that even the smallest among them could shape the future.

Taking a deep breath, Elara began to speak.

"The night of the Eternal Moon was unlike any other," she said, her voice steady but filled with emotion. "It was a time when the boundaries between the mortal and divine realms were blurred, when the gods who had once walked among us returned to claim their power. It was a time of chaos, of danger, but also of great sacrifice and bravery."

As she spoke, she told them of the prophecy, of the journey that had taken her from the safety of the village to the farthest reaches of the world. She spoke of the old gods—Nyxos, the Night God, who had sought to plunge the world into eternal darkness, and the others who had tried to reclaim their dominion over mortals. She told them of the battles fought in the shadows, of the trials she had faced, and of the friends she had lost along the way.

The villagers listened in silence, their faces rapt with attention. Even the children, who had once thought of the gods as nothing more than stories, seemed to sense the gravity of what had happened. Elara could see the awe in their eyes, the way they clung to her every word, as if they, too, were part of the story.

When she spoke of Ilyana's sacrifice, her voice faltered, and for a moment, she had to pause, her throat tight with emotion. But she pressed on, telling them of the ritual that had restored balance, of the price that had been paid to save the world.

"Ilyana gave her life to complete the ritual," Elara said softly, her eyes glistening with unshed tears. "She knew what had to be done, and she did it without hesitation. Because of her, the Eternal Moon has set, and the balance between the realms has been restored."

There was a heavy silence after she spoke, the weight of her words settling over the crowd like a blanket. For a long moment, no one spoke, the only sound the crackling of the fire and the distant murmur of the wind through the trees.

Finally, Liora stepped forward, her expression solemn but filled with respect. "The story of the Eternal Moon will be remembered, Elara. And so will the sacrifices made to save us all."

Elara nodded, though her heart still ached with the loss of Ilyana. "It's not just my story. It belongs to all of us. The choices we make, the sacrifices we're willing to endure... they shape the world we live in."

Liora's eyes gleamed with understanding, and she smiled gently. "You've learned much on your journey, child. The gods may be powerful, but it's our choices that define us."

Elara smiled faintly, though the weight of everything she had experienced still pressed down on her. "Yes. And I've learned that the power of choice is stronger than any prophecy."

The villagers began to disperse, some returning to their homes while others lingered by the fire, their faces filled with quiet contemplation. Elara stood by the fire for a while longer, watching as the flames flickered and danced, casting shadows that seemed to shift and move in the night.

Dorian approached her, his expression solemn. "You did well, Elara. The village needed to hear your story."

Elara nodded, though her heart was still heavy. "I just hope they understand the lessons we've learned. That the balance between the mortal and divine realms isn't something to take for granted."

"They will," Dorian said softly. "You've shown them that even the smallest among us can make a difference."

Elara smiled faintly, though the ache in her chest remained. "I just wish Ilyana were here to see it."

Dorian's expression softened, and he placed a comforting hand on her shoulder. "She is here, Elara. In every choice we make, in every life we help rebuild... she's with us."

Elara closed her eyes, letting the words wash over her. He was right. Ilyana's sacrifice hadn't been in vain. Her memory would live on, not just in Elara's heart, but in the world they had saved. The balance had been restored, and though the connection between mortals and the divine remained, it was now one of cooperation, not domination. The gods would no longer seek to control the world of mortals, but rather to guide and protect them, as it had always been meant to be.

As the night deepened, Elara turned her gaze to the sky. The moon, now back to its natural phase, hung high above them, a reminder of the journey she had undertaken, the battles she had fought, and the sacrifices that had been made.

The Night of the Eternal Moon had passed, but its legend would live on.

The whispers of the gods were still there, soft and distant, guiding her as they had done before. But now, those whispers no longer held the weight of prophecy or power. They were gentle, full of possibilities, a reminder that the future was not set in stone.

Elara knew that her journey was far from over. There were still many challenges ahead, many lives to help rebuild. But as she gazed at the sky, the weight of the past lifted just a little, and she felt a sense of peace wash over her.

The world had changed, and so had she. But in that change, there was hope. The legend of the Eternal Moon would be passed down through generations, a tale of bravery, sacrifice, and the delicate balance between the mortal and divine realms.

And as Elara stood beneath the stars, she knew that the future was full of possibilities—possibilities that she, and the world, would shape together.

The legend was not an ending, but a beginning.

The beginning of a new era.

Don't miss out!

Visit the website below and you can sign up to receive emails whenever Patrick William Lee publishes a new book. There's no charge and no obligation.

https://books2read.com/r/B-A-FLRYB-LYAZE

BOOKS2READ

Connecting independent readers to independent writers.

Did you love *The Night of the Eternal Moon*? Then you should read *The Last Sorcerer*[1] by Patrick William Lee!

The Last Sorcerer takes readers on an epic journey through a kingdom where magic reigns and power is coveted. Aelor, a gifted sorcerer born under mysterious circumstances, embarks on a path of discovery, loyalty, and ultimately, betrayal. Under the guidance of his master, Aelor's choices lead him deeper into dark magic, setting the stage for a prophecy of treachery. As he rises in power, a lost heir emerges, threatening to restore balance. This gripping tale explores the cost of ambition, the corrupting influence of power, and the ultimate price of betrayal.

---

1. https://books2read.com/u/bOdAd0

2. https://books2read.com/u/bOdAd0

About the Author

Patrick William Lee is a renowned author celebrated for his enchanting tales of magic and wonder. Specializing in the genres of fairy tales, folk tales, legends, and mythology, Patrick weaves stories that transport readers to fantastical realms where the impossible becomes reality. With a deep love for folklore and a talent for crafting timeless narratives, his books captivate the imaginations of readers young and old. When he's not writing, Patrick enjoys exploring ancient forests, studying mythical creatures, and sharing his passion for storytelling with audiences around the world. His works continue to inspire and delight, leaving a lasting impact on the world of literature.

9 798822 464074